The Deadly Curse
of Toco-Rey

THE COOPER KIDS ADVENTURE SERIES®

The Deadly Curse of Toco-Rey
The Secret of the Desert Stone

(Available from Crossway Books)

Trapped at the Bottom of the Sea
The Tombs of Anak
Escape from the Island of Aquarius
The Door in the Dragon's Throat

Look for more books to come in the Cooper Kids Adventure Series® from Word*kids!*

The Cooper Kids Adventure Series®

The Deadly Curse of Toco-Rey

Frank E. Peretti

WORD PUBLISHING
Dallas·London·Vancouver·Melbourne

Unless otherwise indicated, Scripture quotations are from the *International Children's Bible, New Century Version,* copyright © 1983, 1986, 1988.

Managing Editor: Laura Minchew
Project Editor: Beverly Phillips

Library of Congress Cataloging-in-Publication Data

Peretti, Frank E.
    The deadly curse of Toco-Rey / Frank E. Peretti.
      p.   cm. — (The Cooper Kids Adventure Series® ; 6)
    "Word kids!"
    Summary: While on a quest to save a piece of history, Jay, Lila, and their father encounter hostile natives and ancient evil forces in the jungles of Central America.
    ISBN 0-8499-3644-6
    [1. Supernatural—Fiction. 2. Jungles—Fiction.
3. Adventure and adventurers—Fiction.] I. Title.   II. Series:
Peretti, Frank E. The Cooper Kids Adventure Series® ; 6.
PZ7.P4254De   1996
[Fic]—dc20   96–15641
                                                                       CIP
                                                                        AC

Printed in the United States of America

96 97 98 99 00 RRD 9 8 7 6 5 4

ONE

Chico Valles, machete in hand, hacked his way along the narrow trail, oblivious to the constant chatter of cicadas and the raucous screams of tropical birds. Sweat trickled down his stubbled face. The thick, encroaching jungle pressed in on him from every direction. It reached with limbs, slapped with leaves, grabbed with vine tendrils. He forced it back with his machete and pressed on as he did every day, running errands for Basehart the American.

Finally he reached the clearing where the Corys had set up their camp. He stopped.

The camp looked deserted. The large tent sagged a bit as if a pole had broken. Cookware, clothing, and food were strewn about under the blue tarpaulin lean-to. The wooden camp chairs and portable table were overturned by the fire pit. A portable camp stove lay on its side, bent and broken, and orchids now lay scattered on the ground, spilled from a vase. Except for the noises of the jungle, Chico heard no sound. Except for the slow crawl of an iguana on a limb overhead, he saw no movement.

Chico tightened his grip on the machete.

"Kachakas," he muttered, his eyes darting about. Then he called, "Hello! Señor Cory!"

No answer.

Steeling his nerves, Chico took a few cautious steps forward, emerging from the jungle with the machete outstretched. He watched every direction for hidden dangers, lurking enemies. He could detect no sign of another human being—at least none still alive.

Then he heard a low, garbled hissing from the tent. A snake? He instinctively drew the machete back, ready to strike. Then he inched forward, trying to get a view through the tent's open flap.

The inside of the tent appeared to have been raided by wild animals. Blankets, sleeping bags, books, charts, and tools were scattered everywhere. The tent fabric had been torn, and one of the support poles was indeed broken.

"Señor Cory!"

Again, no answer. Chico walked closer and stuck his head into the tent.

He found the source of that strange hissing sound. A handheld two-way radio lay on the floor, the case broken and splintered, its dial still glowing. Had someone tried to call for help? Where were they now?

Chico ducked into the shadowy interior, his feet shuffling through scattered clothing and trodden papers.

"Señor—"

His eyes caught a sparkling, golden glow in one corner, and he stared, spellbound. *"El tesoro,"* he whispered. The treasure.

On a steel footlocker stood a tall, ornately

2

engraved vase of gold, several golden cups, a gold jeweled necklace, and small, golden statues of ancient gods and warriors. They all glistened as if newly polished in the faint light that came through the doorway.

Chico took a furtive look outside, then reached down to grab the vase.

The glistening, golden surface felt slick and gooey.

And then it felt like fire. He yanked his hand away with a cry of pain and was horrified to find thin yellow slime on his palm and fingers. It began to penetrate his skin, bubbling and fizzing, burning like millions of red-hot needles.

He frantically wiped his hand on a blanket, then tried to find some water, anything to remove the slime. Searing pain flashed up his arm and he began to scream.

So great was his terror and agony that he didn't see the shadowy figure appear in the doorway, crouching like a lion. When it leaped upon him, the impact jarred him senseless.

The birds cried out, thundering from the treetops. The cicadas cut their song short. The iguana disappeared around the trunk of the big tree.

The tent came alive, lurching and bulging this way and that. Chico's screams mingled with the eerie, cougarlike snarls of his attacker.

At the Langley Memorial Art Museum in New York City, Dr. Jacob Cooper, hat in hand, strolled quietly through the Hall of Kings. Statues, busts, masks, and relief carvings of ancient kings glowered at him from their pedestals along both sides of the vast marble hall.

"Dr. Cooper?" A small man in a dark suit came close and looked up at him.

Jacob Cooper looked down with curiosity. "Mr. Stern?"

The little man smiled. "Mr. Wendell. I work for Mr. Stern. Please come with me."

Dr. Cooper followed him to the end of the hall and through an unmarked door into a large workroom and archive. Shelves lined the walls from floor to ceiling, all loaded down with books, documents, and historical artifacts. In the center of the room stood a large worktable where artifacts were restored and prepared for display.

A gray-haired, well-dressed man sat at the table. He rose when Jacob Cooper entered the room. "Dr. Jacob Cooper?"

Dr. Cooper reached across the table and shook his hand. "Mr. Stern?"

"Thank you for coming." Mr. Stern looked at his associate, who took his cue and left the room. Then Mr. Stern asked, "You *are* alone?"

"Yes, and no one knows of our meeting, just as you requested."

Mr. Stern smiled. "I apologize for the secrecy, but your fame goes before you. And I have reason to believe certain interests would not be happy to see you involved in our little project. Please, have a seat."

Dr. Cooper sat at the big table and Mr. Stern returned to his seat opposite. He rested his hand on an old leather carrying case. "Dr. Cooper, the matters we are about to discuss are of a delicate nature. Human lives are at stake . . . and I'm afraid some have already perished. Have you heard of the lost city of Toco-Rey?"

Jacob Cooper probed his memory. "A legendary city full of treasure somewhere in Central America?"

Mr. Stern brightened, nodding his head. "Toco-Rey is believed to have been built by the Oltecas, who thrived during the decline of the Mayan empire and vanished into history almost 600 years before Columbus."

Dr. Cooper wrinkled his brow. "I've heard a little about it from a treasure hunter who seemed rather obsessed with the place."

"Ben Cory?"

Dr. Cooper smiled. "So you've met him?"

Stern's face grew solemn as he announced, "I'm afraid *he* is one who has died, Dr. Cooper."

Jacob Cooper was saddened by the news but not entirely surprised. "What happened?"

"He was working for us, searching out the lost city, and—" Mr. Stern's eyes grew wide with excitement, "we believe he found it! He and his crew brought artifacts out of the jungle: gold, jewelry, jade, sculpture. Cory was elated, and so were we. But soon after, he and his party were ambushed in their camp and killed. Every last artifact was stolen. We think the local natives, the Kachakas, are responsible. They claim to be descendants of the Oltecas, charged with guarding the city from outsiders."

5

"Foreign treasure hunters, in other words."

"Not in this case!" Mr. Stern countered. "Ben Cory was hired by the Langley Museum, and his quest was not just for treasure but also for knowledge, for history itself. Here. Let me show you." Mr. Stern flipped the leather case open and carefully drew out some old parchments and a worn, cracked leatherbound logbook. "The museum acquired these recently: the journal and maps of José de Carlon, an early Spanish explorer who went to Mexico shortly after Hernán Cortés had finished his conquests. José de Carlon wasn't much of a soldier or conqueror; he was too preoccupied with treasure hunting. Rumors of a lost city, the final stronghold of Kachi-Tochetin, king of the Oltecas, lured him south."

Mr. Stern carefully unrolled one of the brittle, aging maps as Dr. Cooper leaned over the table for a careful look.

"See here? The map shows his route through the jungles to the lost city, and he even marked out where the ruins are. According to his journal, he and his men found Toco-Rey in 1536, six centuries after the city was deserted. Ben Cory and his men used this map to find the treasure, but they were killed before we could find out how, or where."

Dr. Cooper could see where this was going. He fidgeted a little and sighed. "Mr. Stern . . . I'm an archaeologist. Perhaps another treasure hunter . . ."

Mr. Stern leaned forward, intense. "Dr. Cooper, treasure hunting is exactly what we are trying to *prevent!* For years, the ruins of the Mayas have been

6

ravaged and looted by souvenir seekers, and now that Toco-Rey has been found, the same thing could happen there. We could lose a priceless store of Oltecan history and culture to looters—unless we find the treasure first and rescue the artifacts. I know you are a man who cares about such things. I know you would want to preserve history."

Jacob Cooper took a moment to consider. As founder of the Cooper Institute for Biblical Archaeology, he had devoted his life to preserving the past. It had vital lessons it could teach about the present and the future. Saving another piece of history from treasure hunters, black marketeers, and greedy collectors would certainly be in keeping with his and the Institute's goals. "So," he said at length, "you want me to pick up the trail where Ben Cory left off?"

Mr. Stern nodded. "You can follow the maps and notes of José de Carlon, just like Ben Cory did. With your skill and expertise, it should be no problem at all to retrace Cory's route to the treasure."

"No problem at all?" Dr. Cooper leaned back, his fingers lightly drumming his chin. "There's just one thing I'd like to understand. . . ."

"Yes?"

"If José de Carlon found this treasure, why is it still there? Why didn't he carry it off?"

Mr. Stern hesitated, as if unprepared for the question, then sighed. "You may as well know. In his journal, José de Carlon comes across as a very superstitious man. He was afraid of booby traps, magical curses, ancient evil forces. He and his men actually dug their own tunnel into the tomb of Kachi-Tochetin in the hope that they could sneak in secretly and evade any curses or traps." Then he added, "Apparently they didn't succeed."

Dr. Cooper had to prod him to continue. "Go on."

Mr. Stern gave an awkward chuckle and tried to shrug off his words even as he spoke. "He says his men found the treasure, but they all went mad, became like raving animals, and killed each other. He barely got away alive and left the treasure behind, convinced there was a curse on it." Mr. Stern chuckled and shrugged again. "So the treasure is still there, untouched for centuries."

"And guarded by a bizarre curse?"

Mr. Stern leaned over the table, lowering his voice. "Dr. Cooper, we both know this will be no picnic. Of course there are dangers: thick jungle, poisonous snakes, hostile natives. The area is remote, and we can expect little or no government assistance or protection. And . . . well, who knows? Kachi-Tochetin was a fierce, marauding warrior. He conquered peoples and cities all over ancient Mexico and Central America, sacrificing and slaughtering thousands. His treasure is undoubtedly the loot he stole from those he conquered. So maybe the tomb *is* booby trapped somehow. As for a curse . . . well, I understand you are a man of prayer, so I assume you aren't bothered by such things."

Jacob Cooper smiled. "I've run into more than my share of curses and hexes and magic spells, and my God has been greater than all of them."

Mr. Stern drew a deep breath. "Dr. Cooper, you are our last hope. Can we count you in?"

"Welcome to Basehart City," said the handsome, white-haired man in the white shirt and broad straw hat. He could have been a wealthy plantation owner or an English gentleman, so refined was his manner. "This is without a doubt the finest vacation resort in the entire jungle—excluding all the others, that is. I'm the founder, Dr. Armond Basehart."

Dr. Cooper climbed out of the jeep and shook Basehart's hand. "Dr. Jacob Cooper, and this is my daughter, Lila. That's my son, Jay."

Lila Cooper, thirteen, got out of the jeep and stretched. Removing her straw hat, she wiped a slick mixture of sweat and mosquito repellent from her brow. Like her father and brother, she was wearing light clothing. She'd braided her long blond hair to keep it off her neck. Even so, the tropical jungle felt hot, sticky, and uncomfortable.

And Basehart City was nothing to admire. Within a small, tight clearing surrounded by a solid wall of jungle were three travel trailers parked in a U shape. A large blue tarpaulin stretched between them. Two native huts with stick walls and thatched roofs and two mud-spattered trucks completed the encampment. It had taken the Coopers a full day's journey to get here, riding over miles and miles of bumpy, muddy road through jungle so thick they could only see a few feet into it. They were a day's journey from the nearest flushing toilet.

Lila smiled a tired smile. *This is going to be better than I thought.*

Jay Cooper, fourteen, was still working on being tall like his father, but he was already strong. And he had his father's sandy blond hair and piercing blue eyes. He took a moment to study the surroundings, feeling the curious stares of the native workers. One was butchering what looked like a pig, another was building a lean-to, and the third was burning trash in a small fire. Directly above, the treetops formed a tight, dark frame around a circular patch of blue sky. Brightly colored birds perched in the branches, screaming at one another in voices continually alarmed about something.

Adventure, he thought. *I can just feel it!*

Armond Basehart took them to the dismal-looking trailer that faced his own across the small, makeshift courtyard. "This is our special guest suite. You'll have running water from the trailer's supply tank—Juan and Carlos will keep it filled for you—and a limited supply of electricity from the trailer's batteries. Please try to conserve it. There's an outhouse behind this trailer, but check it for snakes before you use it. As you can see, we provide only the best accommodations for our guests."

Dr. Cooper looked around the inside of the trailer. It was a twenty footer, with a small kitchenette, dinette table and benches, a closet-sized shower, and beds for at least four. Everything looked old and well traveled. But in this rugged country, these *were* luxurious accommodations. He set down his duffel bag. "We'll take it."

They got settled, and then Dr. Basehart filled them in. "Ben Cory, his brother, John, and their associate, Brad Frederick, had a camp set up about a half mile farther into the jungle, closer to the ruins. I chose to stay here in the main camp with the supplies, the workers, the vehicles, and my lab, of course. Besides serving as the team doctor, I am also doing a little private research, collecting and categorizing some of the local fungi."

Dr. Cooper spotted a narrow, new trail leading into the jungle. "Is that the trail to the Corys' camp?"

"It is. I can have Tomás take you there now if you like."

Jacob Cooper reached into the trailer and pulled out his gunbelt. "Jay! Lila! Let's go!"

Dr. Basehart touched him on the shoulder. "Uh, Dr. Cooper . . . you may not want your children to go. As you probably know, the Corys died violently."

Dr. Cooper considered that as he checked his .357 and slid it into the holster at his side. "Where are the bodies now?"

"We buried them not far from their camp."

Jay and Lila emerged from the trailer, ready to get started.

Dr. Cooper reassured his host, "My kids haven't seen everything, but they've seen enough in our travels. They'll be all right."

Dr. Basehart accepted that, then he called to one of the workers. "Tomás!"

"Sí, señor." Tomás came running.

Dr. Basehart introduced them. "Dr. Cooper, Jay,

Lila, this is Tomás Lopez, my assistant." Tomás shook their hands, grinning a toothy grin, happy to be of service. "He'll take you to see the Corys' camp and answer any questions you have."

Tomás's smile vanished, and he looked wide-eyed at his boss. "Señor Basehart . . . is that such a good idea?"

Basehart became quite impatient. "Tomás, I will not have this discussion again with you! There is nothing to be afraid of!"

"But—" Tomás got a cold glare from his boss and cut short his protest. "Muy bien."

Dr. Basehart told the Coopers, "When you return, I'll show you the video tape the Corys made of their findings. It will give you an idea of what they were doing and possibly give you some clues to follow."

Dr. Cooper nodded. "I'll definitely want to see that."

Tomás eyed the holster on Dr. Cooper's hip. "Ah, you have a gun. That is good. Come with me."

Tomás stopped by his hut to grab a rifle and a machete, then he led the Coopers down the trail into the jungle. The thick vegetation closed in around them, making them stoop and push branches aside. The thick canopy overhead choked out the daylight.

Tomás was upset. For several minutes he muttered to himself in Spanish, and then he shared his thoughts with the Coopers in English. "This is not a safe place! It is magic, you know. *Bad* magic. We should not even be here!"

They journeyed farther into the deep jungle, surrounded by noisy birds and cicadas, until finally they saw a bluish glint ahead. Tomás slowed his pace and crouched as if sneaking up on something. The Coopers instinctively crouched as well and followed.

"There," Tomás whispered, gesturing toward a small clearing with his machete. From the edge of the clearing, they could see the ragged tent and blue tarpaulin lean-to, the camp where the Corys had been ambushed. "Before we go farther, I will warn you: You will see blood inside, and terror, and signs of Kachaka magic. The Corys came this far, and now they are dead." He looked directly at them. "There is a curse on this place. If you go farther, you may end up dead too. So decide!"

TWO

The Coopers were cautious but not afraid. With firm resolve, they stepped into the clearing, moving carefully, observing every detail. Tomás followed behind, sticking close, eyes wary, the rifle and machete ready.

The camp was a disaster area with camp chairs knocked over, the tent half collapsed, the camp stove overturned on the ground, food and supplies torn, scattered, and spilled everywhere. It had been a mess to begin with, and now scavenging animals had made it even worse.

Jay found a small, thin reed stuck in a tree trunk near the tent. "Dad."

Jacob Cooper went over and examined it without touching it. "Poison dart."

Tomás nodded warily. "The Kachakas. They use poison darts and blowguns. The poison kills in seconds."

Lila noticed the overturned vase and scattered orchids. "I bet these orchids were beautiful before they wilted."

Tomás smiled crookedly. "Americans. They

14

would pay lots of money for such flowers in their own country. Here, we see them everywhere."

"All the tools are still in place," Dr. Cooper observed, checking the collection of shovels, picks, brush hooks, and metal detectors near a tree. He found a large wooden chest, eased the lid open, and whistled his amazement at the contents.

Jay came to look. "What is it?"

"Explosives," said his father. "That always was Ben Cory's style: Just blast away and get the treasure out, never mind the historical value of the site." He closed the lid gently, with great respect for what the chest held. "Let's have a look in that tent."

The tent had half-fallen. Dr. Cooper found a long stick near the firepit and stuck it into the tent to prop up the roof.

"We'll have to gather up all these notes," he said, indicating the papers scattered on the floor. "We need to know everything the Corys knew."

"Careful!" Jay cautioned, pointing to another poison dart that poked through the tent.

Lila picked up one of the sheets of note paper. It was heavy, sticky, and stained red. "Euuughh."

"I told you there would be blood," said Tomás from outside where he nervously stood guard. "The Corys were slaughtered in this tent."

There was blood, all right, spattered on the floor of the tent, on the clothes, work boots, and gear. The Corys *had* died violently.

Jacob Cooper kept his tone calm and even. "Lila, I think we need one more set of eyes and ears outside. We don't need any surprises."

Lila welcomed the idea. Her face pale, she quickly ducked outside.

Dr. Cooper drew a deep breath and spoke to Jay. "Let's do it."

He and Jay began gathering up the notes, drawings, charts, and maps from the tent floor, separating them from the shirts, socks, bottles, and boxes lying everywhere.

Jay spotted a small notebook partially hidden under some wadded up rags. He reached for it then jerked his hand away, his heart racing. "Dad!"

Dr. Cooper's hand went to his gun. "What is it?"

Lila poked her head in. "What is it?"

Jay backed away from the pile. "There's something under those rags."

The rags were wiggling and heaving.

Lila stifled a cry of fear, pressing her hand over her mouth as Tomás stuck his head into the tent. "Qué pasa?"

"I think we've got a snake in here," said Dr. Cooper. "Stand back." He found a piece of broken tent rod and extended it toward the rags, prodding them slightly. The motion stopped. He slowly lifted the rags.

They saw a fluttering, a flash of dull yellow and heard a tiny, shrill scream!

Lila screamed as well, and Jay and Dr. Cooper ducked. A strange, fluttering, flapping shape shot from the rags and began banging and slapping against the walls of the tent like a trapped bird.

Tomás hollered, "Get back! Get back!" and plunged into the tent, swinging his machete. The thing continued to fly, land, leap, bump against the tent, and flutter over their heads. Lila jumped away from the tent; Jay and his father dropped to the floor. Tomás kept swinging.

SPLAT! The machete finally made contact and the animal landed on the tent floor, fluttering like a wounded bird, flopping about like a fish.

Jay and Dr. Cooper got to their feet. Tomás stood over the thing, machete only inches from it, venting his supercharged emotions in rapid, coarse Spanish. They started to approach.

Tomás shot his hand out toward them. "Stay back! Wait!"

The thing finally stopped flopping and Tomás relaxed, breathing in deep breaths of relief. He beckoned to them, and they approached as Lila stuck her head back into the tent, eyes wide with curiosity.

Tomás pointed at the thing. "*Caracol volante.* We call them carvies. A flying slug."

"A *what?*" Jay exclaimed, still trembling a bit.

"Amazing!" added Dr. Cooper, bending for a closer look. "I've heard such tall tales about them! I never thought they were real!"

"They are not seen very often," said Tomás. "They are rare and only come out at night."

There at Tomás's feet, a loathsome little creature lay dead. It looked like a big garden slug, about six inches long, with a yellowish, slimy hide. But instead of feelers, it had tiny, black ratlike eyes. On either side of its soft, gooey body, glistening skin extended outward to form winglike fins, much like those of a

17

stingray. Tomás used the tip of his machete to snag a fin and extend it to show the Coopers.

Lila came in and peered over everyone's shoulder. "Wow . . ."

"Not a slug, actually," Dr. Cooper explained to his kids. "But it *is* a member of the mollusk family—and one of the strangest."

"Don't touch it!" Tomás warned. "The slime is deadly poison, the same the Kachakas use to tip their darts." He glanced quickly around the tent. "See? There is slime on the tent fabric and on some of the clothes. Be very careful. It will burn through your skin and kill you."

Without having to be told, they all backed carefully out of the tent and then checked their clothes for any traces of slime.

"Most of it has dried up, which is good," said Tomás. "It has to be fresh to burn through your skin."

"What was that thing doing in there?" Dr. Cooper wondered.

"It was probably attracted by the blood. Carvies are flesh eaters: They feed on dead animals, blood, meat of any kind. There were probably others in the tent last night. This one decided to sleep under the rags."

Jay shook his head. "So that's one more thing to worry about—besides the biting insects, the poisonous snakes, and the hostile natives."

"How far away is the Kachaka village?" asked Dr. Cooper.

Tomás shrugged. "I have never been there. It's

somewhere beyond the ruins, I think. But the Kachakas claim all this land, and they aren't happy that we're here." Tomás cocked his head toward the woods just beyond the camp. "The Corys have already learned that. Come this way."

They followed him into a small clearing. There, marked with crude wooden crosses, were three graves. "Ben Cory, John Cory, Brad Frederick," said Tomás, pointing out each one. "Gone in one night, their treasure stolen."

Jacob Cooper had seen enough. "All right, let's get these materials back to the compound and see if we can sort them out. And then we'll watch a movie."

After hiking back to the compound, they ate a hurried dinner—roast pig cooked over the fire by Tomás's coworkers—and then settled into their trailer to examine the notes left behind by the Corys. In the light of a gas lantern, Jay and Lila carefully cleaned, sorted, and stacked the materials, and Dr. Cooper laid them out in orderly fashion on the dinette table to study them.

"Hmm . . . ," he said, using a small flashlight to illuminate some hard-to-read areas. "I'm impressed. The Corys put a lot of time into mapping out the ruins. Look here: Toco-Rey was built on top of the ruins of a previous city, which was built on top of the ruins of a previous city, and so it goes. It's only about a mile square and used to be walled like a fortress. It would have been easy for Kachi-Tochetin to hole up there for years and defend his loot from his enemies."

Lila spotted a dark, square shape someone had drawn near the map's eastern edge. "I'll bet that's the burial temple Ben Cory wrote about." She leafed through a pile of freshly scrubbed materials and pulled out a ragged-edged notebook. "Yeah, take a look at this."

Dr. Cooper quickly flipped through the notebook, then compared the scribblings and sketches with the map on the table. "Lila, you're right on the money. It *is* the burial temple. Ben Cory guessed they'd find the treasure there. He figured since Kachi-Tochetin was such a gold-hound, the old king probably had himself buried with it."

Jay produced some smaller maps, roughly drawn with pencil and now faintly bloodstained. "I think these maps lay out the route they followed to get to the burial temple."

Dr. Cooper laid the maps out on the table and traced the route with his finger. "Looks like the same route José de Carlon took centuries ago: up the slope past the waterfall . . . across the swamp . . . through the main gates of the city . . . around the Pyramid of the Moon and due north up the Avenue of the Dead . . ."

"Avenue of the *Dead?*" said Lila.

"Sounds inviting," quipped Jay.

A knock on the screen door startled them. "Hello. How goes the battle?" It was Armond Basehart.

"I'm encouraged," replied Dr. Cooper. "The

Corys kept a thorough record. We should be able to retrace their route first thing tomorrow morning."

Basehart was visibly pleased. "Good enough! Well, I have the Corys' video ready. Come on over and have a look."

Outside Basehart's trailer, Tomás yanked the starter rope on a portable gas generator. Inside the trailer, the electric lights came on and so did a ten-inch color television perched in Basehart's tight little living room. Basehart had the Corys' palm-sized video camera wired to the television, and after fumbling a little with various switches and buttons, finally got the tape rolling and a picture on the screen.

The Coopers leaned forward as one person, gazing intently, and immediately recognized the Corys' camp in the jungle. The camera jiggled, panning the camp, showing the tent, the campfire, the table and chairs. Even the vase of orchids was standing upright on the table, the orchids in much fresher condition. "And this is our tent, and over here we have the fire, and here's our nice outdoor dining room . . ." went the cameraman's prattle, the kind of silly stuff that always goes with home movies.

Then a young man appeared from behind the tent, carrying some firewood. He was tall and thin, with a smile so wide and teeth so white it caught your eye. "And here's Brad, doing the chores . . . ," continued the narrator.

Brad shot back, "Did you get a shot of the treasure?"

"No," the cameraman answered, "I'm doing establishing shots here."

Then came a voice from off-camera, "Well, get the camera over here, Ben. You're wasting Mr. Stern's time."

"Ehh, everybody's gotta be a director." The camera did a quick, blurry pan to the table near the firepit, and then it picked up the glimmer of gold—a lot of gold.

"Will you look at that!" Jay exclaimed in a near whisper.

"Here's just a preview of what we found," said Ben the cameraman, zooming in for a close-up of incredible gold artifacts: an ornately engraved vase of gold at least two feet tall, several golden plates and cups, a necklace of gold and jewels, and at least a dozen golden figurines only a few inches tall.

Hands entered the picture, holding another vase and wiping it down with a rag. "We found these in the tomb and carried them out through the tunnel. Everything is pretty dusty down there. We wore dust masks, but still came out of that place all dirty. No problem though. See here? It just takes a rag to clean the artifacts and they polish right up."

The camera zoomed back to show John Cory, a long-haired, bare-chested man. John set the vase down and picked up some of the small figures to show to the camera, wiping them some more with his rag. "We have here tiny figurines of a bird-god, possibly another form of Quetzalcoatl, the feathered serpent god."

Ben, from behind the camera, explained, "These were stationed all around the walls of the room like

22

sentries, probably to guard the treasure from spirits of the dead, maybe even from living enemies—"

John butted in, "There were other guards there too, but they weren't much help."

Ben laughed. "No, they sure weren't. We're going to take the camera and some lights with us tomorrow. We should get some great shots of the treasure room and the tunnel—"

"If we can get past the slugs," Brad quipped, coming into the picture and turning some of the artifacts for better viewing.

John agreed, "Yeah, the carvies can be a bit of a problem. They like the tunnels and underground areas just like bats like caves, but we're dealing with it."

"We'll retrace our route for you," came Ben's voice from off-camera, "which closely matches the route taken by José de Carlon more than four hundred years ago."

"The old guy was right about the treasure," said Brad.

"But wrong about the curse," said John, indicating the treasure on the table. "I mean, here's the treasure, and here we are, safe and sound."

"Okay," said Ben, "let's get this stuff into the tent." Then, in a louder, announcer's voice, "Stay tuned, folks, for tomorrow's exciting venture into the burial temple of King Kachi-Tochetin!"

The television screen went to snow.

Dr. Basehart turned it off. "That's it. They were ambushed and killed that very night. They never went back."

Dr. Cooper looked at his kids for their reaction.

Lila was troubled. "Is the treasure worth it?"

Her father reflected on the question. "Some people are greedy enough to take the risk. For others, . . ." He sighed. "Well, we should be willing to ask that question more than once on this trip."

"A tunnel," said Jay. "We're definitely looking for a tunnel."

"Perhaps the original tunnel dug by José de Carlon and his men," Dr. Cooper said. "And apparently inhabited by more *caracoles volantes*."

"Oh *great!*" Lila moaned.

Dr. Basehart was quick to say, "But the Corys got around the carvies somehow. They got into the treasure room!"

Dr. Cooper rose to his feet. "And so will we. Let's call it a day and get some shut-eye. We'll confront those poisonous slugs—"

"And snakes," added Lila.

"And hostile natives with poison darts," added Jay.

"Tomorrow," finished Dr. Cooper.

THREE

The night passed slowly, as any night filled with fear and foreboding will. Lila lay in a bed toward the back of the trailer, staring up at the ceiling, listening, thinking. Again and again she replayed the memory of the Corys' blood-spattered tent and the poison darts they had found. Jay, lying very still in the bed across the trailer from her, listened carefully for the sound of footsteps stealing close to the trailer. As he peered out the narrow window, he hoped he wouldn't see the glint of a killer's eyes lingering in the bush. Dr. Cooper wasn't lying down at all. He sat on his bed—the dinette folded down to make one—listening and watching.

Draping a thin blanket around her shoulders, Lila got up and went to her father's side. "Dad, you okay?"

"So far," he said softly. He put his arm around her, giving her a loving squeeze as he looked out the windows again. "It's very quiet out there."

"I can't sleep."

"Neither can I."

"Me neither," came Jay's voice from his bed.

"Which makes me wonder why everyone else can."

Lila bent down and peered out the window as well, seeing no activity, no lights, and hearing no sounds beyond the constant night chatter of the jungle. "Are they all asleep?"

"I think so," said Dr. Cooper. "I just did a little patrolling around the camp without encountering anyone on watch—no sentry, no safeguards at all. If I could do it, then a whole tribe of Kachakas could sneak into this camp and never be noticed. Either Basehart and his men are too dense to get a clue from what happened to the Corys, or . . ."

"Or what?" asked Jay, coming up front to join them.

Jacob Cooper thought a moment, but then he shook his head. "I don't know. It doesn't make sense." He turned from the window to face his kids. "But we have to get some sleep. Let's take turns keeping watch. I'll take the first shift for two hours."

"I'll take the next," said Jay.

"Then me," Lila said with a shrug.

"I'll leave my gun by the door. Each of you keep it beside you on your watch."

And that's how they spent the rest of the night.

The morning air was warm, wet, and full of earthy smells when the Coopers emerged from their trailer. Armond Basehart was already up and active, barking orders to his three men. Tomás and his two friends, Juan and Carlos, appeared moody and somber. They kept their eyes on the jungle as they gathered equipment and crammed provisions and tools into large backpacks.

"Well, good morning," Dr. Basehart greeted them. "Did you sleep well?"

Dr. Cooper couldn't help noticing his host's well-rested, almost chipper demeanor. "Well enough. How about yourself?"

"Just fine, thank you. Well, grab some breakfast and get yourselves ready. The day wears on!"

Jacob Cooper, Jay, and Lila had their backpacks ready. They ate a quick breakfast of fruit juice and granola and then geared up.

Dr. Cooper slipped into his "map vest," which had many deep pockets where he could carry maps and charts close at hand. He neatly tucked the Corys' maps and photocopies of the original de Carlon maps into the pockets, strapped on his revolver and backpack, put on his hat, and was ready to go.

They headed out, Dr. Cooper leading, making their way back along the trail that led to the Corys' campsite. Jay and Lila followed directly behind their father; Dr. Basehart and his three workers followed behind them. As the jungle closed in around them, the mood of the group darkened, and there was little talking. Even Armond Basehart's hurried, commanding manner had fallen away and he, like the others, stole along the trail quietly, eyes wide open and attentive. Tomás's face clearly indicated what was on his mind: Kachakas. Magic. The curse. His two friends, Juan and Carlos, each carried rifles and pointed them every direction they looked as if expecting an enemy behind every tree.

They pressed on through the thick growth like fleas on a dog's back, stepping over, ducking under, and sidestepping the branches and leaves that brushed and raked against them. The sounds of birds and insects made a constant rattle in their ears.

When they reached the camp, they found it further deteriorated, torn, and scattered by another night's visitations of scavenging animals. Tomás, Juan, and Carlos began muttering to each other in Spanish, and Dr. Basehart had to shush them.

Dr. Cooper pulled out Ben Cory's map sketched in pencil, then carefully walked around the camp perimeter until he found the crude trail the Corys had hacked through the jungle. Without a word, he beckoned to the others, and they continued, the jungle closing around them more than ever.

They hiked and crept for another half-mile or so, and then they began to climb a shallow rise. Dr. Cooper consulted his map. So far, everything checked out. Another half-mile should bring them to—

They froze in their tracks. Tomás aimed his rifle up the rise, the barrel quivering in his trembling hand. Dr. Cooper's hand went to the .357 on his hip.

Somewhere out there, deep within the tangle of jungle, something was screaming. It was not the cry of a bird or the howl of a wild dog, but something far more eerie and strange. It rose in pitch, then fell, then rose again, in long, anguished notes of terror, or maniacal rage, or pain . . . they couldn't tell.

It faded, and then it was gone. They stood silently for a long, tense moment, listening. But they heard nothing more.

Dr. Cooper looked to Dr. Basehart for an explanation.

Armond Basehart gave him a blank stare, then he turned to his men. "What was that?" he hissed.

They looked at each other, jabbering in Spanish, then shrugged at him, shaking their heads. "We do not know, señor," said Tomás. "We have never heard that sound before."

Jay and Lila could feel their hearts pounding and took some deep breaths to steady themselves. They watched their father, who remained still, listening, thinking.

Dr. Cooper looked back at his children, then at the rest of the party. "We're going to stay close together, right?"

They all nodded in full agreement. No problem there.

Dr. Cooper turned and continued up the trail without a word. The others followed, climbing the rise, all the more attentive to every sound, every movement around them.

A tree limb moved! Juan swung his rifle around as everyone froze.

A green tree snake, slithering down the limb in a slow, lazy spiral, flicked its long, red tongue at the air. Juan relaxed and exhaled.

The sound of rushing water reached their ears. Jacob Cooper checked his map. "This should be the waterfall."

The waterfall was like a silken veil, dropping about ten feet into a deep pool edged with moss.

"Beautiful!" Lila exclaimed.

"Let's go swimming," Jay wished out loud.

"Let's get out of here," Dr. Basehart urged. "We can't hear if something's sneaking up on us!"

They kept climbing and reached the top of the rise. Like a moat to block their path, swampy land lay before them, stinking with rot, buzzing with black insects. It rippled with the twitches of larvae and the slithering of water snakes. Dry ground was scarce; the crooked, moss-laden trees and clumps of spear grass rose out of the black water as if growing from a mirror.

Dr. Cooper pulled another map from his vest pocket and snapped it open. "We're close. This swamp was probably used as a moat at one time. The city gates are just on the other side." He looked around, searching for something. "The Corys found a way across and are supposed to have marked it."

Jay pointed. "Dad, I think I see a red ribbon over there."

He saw a ribbon tied around a crooked tree branch, and beyond that, another. "Watch your step, everybody."

The ground was soft and spongy beneath their feet. Sometimes they had to walk ankle-deep in the murky water as they moved carefully from a tiny mound of spear grass to a flat stone to a fallen log to a gooshy, muddy island. They zigzagged across the swamp from each red ribbon to the next.

Another scream, this time closer! Lila flinched,

pulling her hands near her face. Tomás spun left, then right, rifle ready, eyes wide with fear.

From within a tall clump of spear grass, a jawless, mossy-green skull stared back at Tomás and he screamed.

Then Juan screamed.

Then Carlos screamed.

"Quiet, you fools!" Dr. Basehart shouted, looking pretty shaken himself.

Dr. Cooper doubled back to have a look and used his machete to brush the spear grass aside. This skull was not alone. Beyond it, in a long, straight row, were several others, all impaled on the ends of poles, and all green with moss. They'd been here a long while.

"Kachaka magic!" Tomás hissed, his voice squeaking with fear.

"What do you make of it, Dr. Cooper?" Dr. Basehart asked.

"Yes, probably Kachakas," Jacob Cooper replied. "This sort of thing is used as a charm to ward off unwelcome spirits—or people. It's a warning, a scare tactic." He shot a glance at the three terrified workers. "Works pretty well."

"Dad," Lila called. "I think I see the ruins."

He hurried to the front of the line again and bent to peer through the jungle growth. Lila was right. Some distance away, a fierce-looking, toothy face of stone, splotchy with moss and lichens, glared back at them through the trees. Just a few more careful moves between red ribbons should get them there.

No one wanted to remain in the swamp with the

skulls, so they made those few careful moves quickly. They stood before the imposing gateposts of Toco-Rey: two basalt pillars carved in the shape of warriors with feathered headdresses, standing at least twenty feet tall. Judging from their snarling expressions, the warriors weren't designed to make visitors feel welcome.

Tomás, Juan, and Carlos got the message. They were ready to turn back right then and there.

Jacob Cooper, however, was fascinated. "Notice the position of the arms. Undoubtedly these pillars used to support a massive wooden gate between them; the warriors' arms served as the top hinges." He referred to his map and then pointed. "And that huge hill you see just beyond the gate is no hill at all, but a man-made pyramid overgrown by the jungle: the Pyramid of the Moon."

Jay and Lila could only stare in amazement. The Pyramid of the Moon rose at least a hundred feet above the jungle floor. Stair-stepped like a huge wedding cake, its chalky, limestone surface was visible only through small gaps in the overgrowth.

"See that small, square temple at the very top?" Dr. Cooper asked, pointing. "The Egyptians built their pyramids to serve as tombs, but the Middle Americans usually built them as gigantic bases for their temples, so they could be closer to their gods."

They proceeded through the gates, walking on soil, moss, and vegetation. Sometimes they could see the flat paving stones that had once formed the main street through Toco-Rey. Jacob Cooper kept an eye on his map as he guided them along. "We go around the Pyramid of the Moon and walk due north up the Avenue of the Dead . . ."

"The Avenue of the Dead!" Tomás exclaimed.

Dr. Cooper tried to comfort him. "José de Carlon named it that, probably because it was the main thoroughfare to the Pyramid of the Sun where they practiced human sacrifice."

"Then the spirits of the dead are here!" Tomás muttered.

"There are no inhabitants here, dead or otherwise!" Dr. Basehart snapped. "Now I'll thank you to control yourselves and do your jobs!"

They circled around the Pyramid of the Moon and found the Avenue of the Dead. A flat, vine-covered expanse, it stretched straight north, about half a mile long and a hundred feet wide. Crumbling stone structures lined either side of it. Some of the buildings were tall enough to be seen above the bushes and trees; some were covered over completely so that they resembled green hedges rather than buildings. At the far end of the avenue stood another man-made mountain, a stair-stepped pyramid with another squarish temple at its peak. This one was even larger and more glorious than the Pyramid of the Moon.

"That would be the Pyramid of the Sun," said Dr. Cooper, "the religious focal point of the city."

As they walked slowly down the Avenue of the Dead, Jay and Lila imagined this street as it might have been over a thousand years ago: filled with bronze-skinned people in brightly feathered garments and jangling gold jewelry, bartering, selling,

33

and herding among the pyramids, temples, and dwellings. They could hear the hum of the marketplace where grains and goods were sold on the stone porches and patios. They could feel the jostling, the pressing of the crowds gathering to gaze up the steep sides of the Pyramid of the Sun at another human sacrifice. These were a beautiful but ruthless people, enslaved by fear, but proud. Now they were gone forever, lost in centuries of time. Were they conquered, or did their culture simply wither away? No one knew.

They reached the base of the Pyramid of the Sun, and Dr. Cooper paused to double-check his maps and notes. "The Pyramid of the Sun stands at the center of the city and could have served as a nice decoy to lure would-be treasure hunters to the wrong place. The real location of the treasure is due east of the pyramid, toward the rising sun . . ." Dr. Cooper looked east and then pointed at one more pyramid, this one rather plain looking, heavily cloaked in green growth, and much smaller than the first two. "That pyramid over there. That's the burial temple of Kachi-Tochetin."

Armond Basehart clapped and rubbed his hands together. "Excellent!"

They walked east, following the narrow trail the Corys had hacked through the thick undergrowth. Already, the jungle had begun to move in again, and the new growth brushed against their bodies.

When they finally came to within a hundred feet of the burial temple, Jacob Cooper stopped to carefully scan the area, look at the latest Cory map, and shake his head. "Well, the first part was easy. Now is where the work begins."

It was obvious that the Corys had done a lot of exploring. A maze of trails and small clearings had been cut in all directions. But that was the problem.

"Which way do we go?" Jay wondered.

Dr. Cooper folded the map and put it in his pocket. "The map doesn't show a thing. Apparently the Corys never got a chance to write down where they found that tunnel."

Lila caught a glint of white among the greenery. "Hey look, more orchids!"

The orchids nodded in full, healthy clusters along a crumbling wall.

"Well, at least that's a confirmation that we're in the right place," said Dr. Cooper. "The Corys had some of those orchids back at their camp."

Lila found the trail the Corys had cut through to the orchids and couldn't resist giving them a sniff to see if they had a scent.

Dr. Cooper began giving out instructions. "Okay, everybody, we're going to split into two groups and work our way around the temple until we meet on the other side. Stay within earshot and keep track of each other in case there's trouble. We need to go everywhere the Corys may have been to find that tunnel into the pyramid. Lila, let's go!"

She hurried back to join them, and then the searching began. Tomás, Juan, and Carlos worked their way to the left; Dr. Basehart and the Coopers ventured off to the right, spreading out, groping, poking, and whacking their way through the undergrowth, sometimes on previously cut trails, sometimes not.

Jay was wielding a machete, widening a channel through growth higher than his head. "Man, you'd think the Corys would have left some markers or something."

Lila was about twenty feet to his right, following a well-chopped, well-traveled path through growth as thick as mattress stuffing and well over her head. "This trail might lead somewhere. It looks like they used it quite a bit. Jay, where are you?"

"I'm over here," he replied, although he wasn't entirely sure where "over here" was.

"Well, can you see the pyramid?"

Jay looked up in several directions, but all he could see were leaves, branches, and vine tendrils. "Dad?"

"Yeah," came Dr. Cooper's voice somewhere ahead of him.

"I think we're lost."

"I can see the pyramid immediately to my left, which would be to your left," his father replied. "I think you're still on course."

"And I'm a bit behind you," came Dr. Basehart's voice. "Let's just keep talking so we can keep tabs on each other."

Jay called, "You hear that, Lila?" No answer. "Lila?"

Lila had come to a wide clearing filled with chopped and fallen brush. She was probing through the debris with her machete. "Jay, I think I may have found something."

Jay stopped whacking. "What?"

Lila used her machete to brush some withering branches aside. Underneath she found a section of low, stone wall. "It's a little wall, kind of like you'd see around a well—you know, it's circular."

Dr. Cooper's voice filtered over the tops of the weeds. "It could be a well. How wide is the circle?"

She began to cut away more growth, gradually uncovering the curve of the wall as it formed a circle about ten feet across. "It's . . . uh, about ten feet across, I think . . ."

But one thing bothered her about this circle: She was standing *inside* it. "Jay?"

"Yeah."

"I think it might be a well. I can feel cold air coming up from below."

Jay heard a cracking sound, then a rustle of leaves and branches—and then a long, echoing scream.

"*LILA!*"

Dead limbs had broken, supporting sticks had snapped, and the thick, centuries-old mat of vegetation had given way under her feet. She was falling into a deep, cold place without light, sliding and bouncing over the slimy stone walls as she tried to grab something, anything.

GOOSH! She slid feet first into something soft, slick, gooey. The well must have a muddy bottom, she thought.

SHRIEKS! FLUTTERING! The stagnant air came alive with a rushing, flittering, flapping, slapping, squeaking.

She screamed and covered her head as countless

little shadows swirled around her, slick and slimy, slapping against her, against each other, against the walls.

She looked up just once and saw the opening she'd fallen through as a circle of daylight alive with hundreds of fluttering, flitting, disk-shaped shadows.

Carvies! The pit was full of them.

FOUR

DAD!" Jay hollered.

But Dr. Cooper had heard his daughter's screams and was already on the way, crashing and thrashing in a straight line through the jungle.

Lila covered her head with her arms as the riled creatures continued to flurry about her, flapping, shrieking, flinging slime from their wingtips. She could feel the slime spattering her everywhere; it was in her hair, on her face, dripping down the back of her neck. "HELP ME!"

Jay reached the well but threw himself to the ground as two frightened, screaming carvies flew out of the pit and over his head. He scurried along the ground and peered over the wall into a black void. "Lila!"

She was screaming for help, her words lost in echoes.

"Dad! This way!" Jay yelled.

Dr. Cooper finally burst into the open. He looked into the pit only a moment before throwing off his backpack and pulling a rope from a side compartment. "Lila! Stay calm! I'm lowering a rope!"

Lila kept her hands around her head as she whimpered in fear and disgust. The stench—the slime, the mold, the carvy droppings—was almost overpowering. Carvies still fluttered and flapped around her. She could feel slime dripping off the end of her nose.

Flop! The rope dropped into the pit with a loop tied in the end. "Put your foot in the loop!" her father called.

She reached for the rope, but lost her balance and fell onto something that clattered, clinked, flipped like tiddly-winks as she landed.

Bones. Leg bones, arm bones, ribs, skulls. The carvies were living in them, crawling on them. They scattered like pigeons when she fell, flying by her face and then . . . where? She could hear them withdraw into a deep, echoing void behind her. She turned her head, still protecting her face with her arms, and could just make out the entrance to a dark passage. A tunnel? Hundreds of carvies had retreated into the cavity, clinging to its walls.

But hundreds more continued to scurry and flop like beached stingrays amid the bones around her. Others hung from the walls of the pit, their backs arched with fear, their beady little eyes locked on her.

She had to get out of there. She righted herself, put her foot in the loop and used both slime-slickened hands to cling to the rope. "Okay."

Dr. Basehart joined Dr. Cooper and Jay, and the three of them hauled in the rope hand over hand until Lila's head popped up through the tangle of weeds and broken branches. She was covered with a thin, greenish slime.

Jay reached out to take her hand, but Dr. Basehart grabbed him. "No. Don't touch her! Just keep pulling on the rope."

"Try to climb out, Lila," said her father. "Yeah, that's it."

She was gasping in fear but used her feet to kick and crawl, and she finally flopped over the wall onto the ground.

Dr. Cooper tore his shirt off. "We've got to get that slime off her! Lila, hold still!" He started wiping the slime from Lila's face with the shirt, speaking gently to her, trying to calm her. Jay took his shirt off as well and started working on one arm while Dr. Basehart used a large handkerchief to work on the other.

"We'll have to get her back to the swamp or the waterfall and wash her off," Dr. Cooper thought out loud. "We'll make a stretcher to carry her."

At that moment, Tomás, Juan, and Carlos burst upon the scene, machetes flashing, rifles ready, hollering in Spanish. At the sight of Lila and the open pit, they figured it all out.

And then they started laughing!

Jacob Cooper wanted to strangle them! "Stop laughing and help us! We've got to get her to the stream to wash her off!"

At that, Juan and Carlos looked at each other and then laughed some more.

Tomás tried to explain. "Señor Cooper, your daughter will be all right. Do not be afraid."

Neither Dr. Cooper nor Jay were ready to believe that. "Help or get out of the way!" Dr. Cooper demanded.

"The slime is green," said Tomás, pointing at Lila and the shirts used to clean her. "These are morning carvies. They are not dangerous."

Cooper upended his backpack and the contents dumped onto the ground. "Grab the rope, Jay, and secure it around the ends of the pack board. We'll make a stretcher."

Tomás kept trying. "Señor Cooper, believe me, if these were yellow evening carvies, Lila would be dead by now." He pointed to Lila once again. She was crying, frantically wiping her face and hair with clothes that had fallen from her father's backpack. "You see? She is alive, full of energy!"

Juan and Carlos added their observations in Spanish, and Tomás translated, "Juan and Carlos say her skin would be burning, and she would be paralyzed and choking to death if the slime were poison."

"We'll talk later," said Cooper, cinching up the last rope on the pack board.

SPLASH! Lila leaped into the pool beneath the waterfall and began rinsing herself off, twirling in the water. Dr. Cooper left a bar of soap, a clean shirt that could serve as a towel, and clean clothes by the pool's edge. Then he joined the others a short distance down the trail. They wanted to give her some privacy, but didn't want to get out of earshot.

"She seems to be all right," he reported, only now beginning to calm.

"What did I tell you?" said Tomás. "The carvies are only dangerous at night when they are yellow. When they are green, they are like pets. They wouldn't hurt anybody."

"Nevertheless," said Basehart, holding up a plastic garbage bag. "I've taken the liberty of bringing back the clothing we used to wipe off the slime. I'd like to analyze it."

"I think that's an excellent idea," said Dr. Cooper. He hollered up the hill, "How's it going, Lila?"

"Okay," came her response.

Jacob Cooper allowed himself a deep sigh of relief. "Thank the Lord."

They sat down to wait.

Dr. Cooper removed his hat, wiped his brow, and asked Tomás, "Now. Would you mind explaining why the carvies are only dangerous when they are yellow?"

Tomás shrugged. "I don't know. In the morning they are green and so we know they are safe. At night, they turn yellow, which means they are deadly."

Dr. Basehart ventured a theory. "I would guess it has something to do with their feeding habits. They forage at night and hide in caves and hollows during the day, like bats. The venom could be for protection from predators while they're out in the open feeding."

Tomás waved his finger in warning. "When they are hungry, they get very mean."

Dr. Cooper wanted to be sure. "But they do go out to forage at night?"

"Sí, señor."

Dr. Cooper thought a moment and then revealed, "Lila says she saw a tunnel down there."

That got everyone's attention.

"A tunnel?" Armond Basehart was ecstatic. "Then we've found it—or rather, Lila has found it! The route to the treasure!"

"Possibly," Jacob Cooper cautioned. "It does seem to fit what the Corys said in the video."

"Yeah," said Jay. "They talked about the carvies being a problem."

"And they said something about guards that weren't helping much." Dr. Cooper smiled at the Corys' dry humor. "Lila found human bones down there. The Corys were probably joking about that."

"Well, there you are!" said Dr. Basehart. "We *have* found it!"

"So . . ." Jay could see a problem immediately. "What about the carvies?"

Just then, Lila came down the trail with wet hair and dry clothes. She was smiling a little, clean but embarrassed by all the fuss she'd caused.

Dr. Cooper put out his hand to help her down the trail. "How are you feeling?"

She was surprised, but greatly relieved. "I feel just fine. I guess Tomás is right."

Her father gave her a hug and so did Jay. Tomás grinned, jubilant.

"So what do we do now?" Jay asked.

Dr. Cooper had already been formulating a plan and announced it to everyone. "We'll come back tonight, after the carvies have gone out foraging and the tunnel is clear. If we time it right, we should finish our business before they come back."

Back at the compound, the Coopers regrouped. They cleaned their slimed clothes, restudied the maps and notes the Corys had left behind, and spent some of the afternoon catching a much-needed siesta in their trailer.

Dr. Armond Basehart said he would nap as well, but he actually spent the time in his laboratory in the third trailer, studying a sample of the green slime he'd taken from Lila. Looking at the sample through his microscope, he nodded to himself. It appeared his theory about the mysterious *caracole volante* was proving correct. Lila Cooper was a very lucky girl indeed.

And he was a very lucky biologist.

When dusk came to the jungle and the treetops looked black against the darkening sky, the Coopers led the group on their second expedition with flashlights in hand and climbing rope in their backpacks. They had extra clothes to cover themselves in case they had a run-in with yellow carvies. The men also carried their weapons again in case they had a run-in with dart-shooting Kachakas.

By the time they reached the gates of Toco-Rey, complete darkness shrouded everything beyond the reach of their flashlights. The pyramids were hidden in the night; the ruins were shrouded under the jungle's thick mantle.

Silently, they stole through the tangled brush until they reached the burial temple of Kachi-Tochetin, now a coal-black silhouette against a tapestry of stars. The birds were silent, but the insects of the jungle were chattering. The still air just above the ruins was quite busy with tiny black bats and, most important, carvies. The slugs were out foraging, just as the Coopers had hoped.

They quickly found the circular pit. Tomás, Juan, and Carlos took positions around it, keeping watch with their rifles. The others knelt in the vines and branches and quietly eased off their backpacks. Even as they prepared to go into the hole they could see a few stray carvies flutter up out of it.

"How many would you estimate were down there?" Dr. Cooper whispered to Lila. None of them wanted to talk too loudly, not knowing what enemies might be lurking in the darkness beyond their sight.

Lila gave a little shrug. "It could have been thousands. They were everywhere."

Dr. Cooper got on his belly and crawled to the wall. Lifting himself just over the top and pushing some vines aside, he clicked his light on and peered into the pit.

The walls glistened with moisture and slime, and far below, the bones Lila had encountered lay in a scattered heap like jackstraws.

"Okay," he called in a quiet voice, digging out a length of rope and tying a loop in the end. "Let's go down and check it out."

"I'll hold a position up here," said Dr. Basehart.

"I hate to admit it, but I suffer terribly from claustrophobia. I would be of little use to you in a dark, cramped tunnel."

Jacob Cooper accepted that. "Okay, you and your men can handle the rope. I'll go first. Jay and Lila, you provide the lights."

Dr. Cooper put on an extra shirt, some gloves, and a scarf to cover most of his face. Then he put his foot in the rope loop, stepped over the wall, and disappeared into the dark, clammy space below as Dr. Basehart and his men lowered him. Jay and Lila shined their flashlights after him, helping to illuminate his way.

He immediately noticed it was cooler down here. It was also dank and smelly. As he rotated on the rope, he shined his light to inspect the walls. The pit was hand dug through soil and limestone, between eight and ten feet across and about fifteen feet deep. The thick layers of dried slime on the walls indicated the carvies had lived here for quite a while. The slime was green, which brought a little comfort. It made sense: The carvies only occupied this place when they were well fed and content.

His foot scraped the wall and knocked some rubble loose. The dirt and rocks fell on the bones with hollow, clinking sounds, and a carvy—this one not so content —hissed and skittered out of the way.

"Hold up!" he called, and they stopped lowering him.

He was only four feet above the bone-covered floor. In the beam of his flashlight he could see two yellow carvies perched on a skull. They didn't like being discovered and hissed and chirped at him, their backs arched. He moved slowly, pulling a plastic spray bottle from his belt. He wished he could predict their behavior.

They bolted from the skull in a mad flutter with piercing little shrieks, moving so fast he had trouble tracking them. They came at him, flapping toward his head. Lashing out, he swatted one away with his flashlight. The other landed on his boot, and he sprayed it with the spray bottle.

The bottle contained a strong salt solution, and the carvy's hide began to melt. It flopped to the floor, squeaking and dying.

The second one came at him again, but he sprayed it in midair and it fell immediately to the floor where it flopped about like a landed fish.

"Jay," he called upward, "your spray bottle idea worked."

"All *right*," Jay called back.

"Dad, be careful!" said Lila.

He hooked the spray bottle back onto his belt and explored the floor of the pit with his flashlight. He saw no more carvies.

"Lower away."

His feet finally came down on the bones, pressing them into the thick layer of carvy droppings that covered the floor. Under his weight, they crumbled. He stepped out of the rope loop and yelled, "Okay, pull it up." Then, turning in the direction of the burial temple, he found the long, narrow tunnel Lila had talked about. Penetrating deep under the earth, it swallowed up the beam of his flashlight in limitless, black distance.

"I see the tunnel," he called. "Come on ahead. It's all clear."

Above, Dr. Basehart and his men pulled the rope back up as Jay motioned to Lila.

She saw his signal, but shook her head. "No, you go first."

It was usually Jay's custom to go last, so he could keep an eye out for his sister. But as he considered her previous encounter with this pit, he understood. "Okay. I'll wait at the bottom for you."

"It's a deal."

Jay pulled a cap down over his head and some gloves on his hands for protection, and Dr. Basehart's men lowered him. Then it was Lila's turn. She put on her drooping, billed, army surplus cap, an extra long-sleeved shirt, and some gloves, and then sat on the wall and swung her legs over the pit.

And then she froze.

"Ready?" asked Dr. Basehart.

Of course she was ready. She was just . . .

She pulled in a deep breath. *Come on, Lila,* she thought. *Get a grip. You can't get scared now, not with everybody watching.* She'd crawled into plenty of deep, dark places with her father and brother. This was nothing new.

But something about this ugly, smelly hole turned her stomach. She felt unsteady. Her hands were trembling.

"Yeah," she finally forced herself to say. "I'm ready."

Mustering just enough courage, she put her weight on the rope and went over the wall, through the tangled leaves and branches . . . and into the dark throat of the pit.

"That's it," came the voice of her father from below. "Easy does it."

She began to rotate on the rope. The walls of the pit moved around her making her dizzy; she felt herself getting sick.

She could hear Jay and her father talking somewhere below her. "Who do you suppose these people were?" Jay asked. "Sacrificial victims, most likely," her father answered, "thrown into this pit after the ceremony on top of the Pyramid of the Sun."

She couldn't look down. "How much farther?" she called, her voice betraying her fear.

"Only six more feet, sis," answered Jay. "No sweat."

Her feet touched down on the crunching, crumbling bones and soft droppings, and she stumbled a little. Jay and Dr. Cooper reached out to steady her.

"You okay?" Dr. Cooper asked. His voice sounded far away.

No, she thought. "Of course I'm okay!" She was still having trouble standing up.

"The ground's firm a few inches down," Dr. Cooper reported.

Strange. To her, the ground seemed to be moving in waves like a water bed.

As her father led the way into the tunnel, he talked in hushed, excited tones, as he always did when he was in the midst of discovery. "I don't think this tunnel was dug by José de Carlon. The tool marks and workmanship are too much like the pit itself. And it's been here so long there are limestone formations. The Oltecas must have chiseled it out."

"Cool," said Jay, following just behind him. "Maybe this was supposed to be a secret passage into the tomb."

"Watch your head and where you step."

There was only room enough for them to squeeze through the tunnel in single file. They had very little headroom thanks to the sharp, menacing stalactites that hung from the ceiling. The floor was no better; jagged stalagmites poked up like daggers everywhere. To Lila, they looked like teeth, and she had the overwhelming impression they were walking into a monster's jaws. The flashlights of her brother and father created sharp, spooky shadows that lunged and leaped all around her head. She kept her light low and her head down. She didn't want to look.

After what seemed like an endless journey through the belly of a monster, Dr. Cooper finally announced, "Okay, there's something up ahead. You see that?"

"Wow! It's got to be the tomb!" said Jay.

Lila stopped. *Tomb.* The very word terrified her. She'd never been terrified of a tomb before, but she was now. She put her hand against the cold limestone wall to steady herself. The tunnel felt like it was pitching, rolling.

Dr. Cooper and Jay had entered a room, or was it a hallway? There was a flat wall directly in front of them, but the room seemed to stretch a great distance to either side of them.

Dr. Cooper shined his light both ways and could see that the hall turned a corner at each end. "This passage might go clear around the base of the pyramid, kind of an outer hallway around a room in the middle."

Back in the tunnel, Lila forced herself to take more steps forward. She dared to look up and saw that her brother and father had found a room of some kind.

"Lookitthe formindiss inscriptonida walllll . . ." she heard her father say.

"Den mebbe idwazda curse dey watogginbout . . ." she thought Jay replied.

She took off her gloves and rubbed her ears. It seemed so noisy in this place. A roaring sound everywhere . . .

Dr. Cooper scanned the relief carvings on the wall. "Yes . . . pictures of the serpent god and human sacrifice. You know, human sacrifices were often dressed up in gold and finery donated by the people. Considering what a greedy scoundrel old Kachi-Tochetin was, I wonder if the priests used this passage to sneak into the pit and strip the dead."

Jay could imagine the scenario. "They kill the victim on the Pyramid of the Sun, throw the body into the pit . . ."

"As a sacred offering to some form of god . . ."

"And then sneak into the pit through this tunnel to get all the gold and jewels for themselves."

"Could be they had quite a scam going here." Dr. Cooper shined his flashlight up and down the long passage. "But if that's true, then there has to be another way in and out."

Jay could hear Lila stumbling in the tunnel behind him and looked back. "Lila?" Her flashlight beam was drooping. She seemed to be staggering. "Hey, Lila, you okay?"

"Okay your minute when it's wider, I'm a gimme . . ." she answered.

Jay reached out and grabbed his father's arm. "Dad . . ."

Dr. Cooper had also heard Lila's response. "Lila? How's it going back there?"

They could only see the beam of her flashlight coming up the tunnel. She didn't answer.

Dr. Cooper shined his light in her face.

She cowered, covering her face with her arms. "NOO! Light now, I'm over inside!"

"She's talking crazy!" Jay exclaimed.

"Something's wrong," said Dr. Cooper. They hurried back into the tunnel. "Lila, hold still, sweetheart, we're coming."

Jacob Cooper had almost reached her, was just about to touch her, when she dropped her arms and he saw her face.

Her skin had turned a pale green. Her eyes were wild, like a savage animal's. She screamed a scream that chilled his blood.

He tried to grab hold of her. "Lila—"

SWAT! She struck him across the face before he even saw it coming, her fingernails gouging him, the power of the blow enough to knock him off balance. He fell backward to the tunnel floor, a sharp stalagmite just missed his rib cage.

"Lila," Jay cried, "what are you doing?"

Her flashlight lay amid the stalagmites, still shining. Far beyond its small circle of light, Jay and Dr. Cooper could hear Lila racing back up the tunnel with incredible speed.

"Did you see her?" Dr. Cooper exclaimed, carefully getting to his feet. "Did you see her face?"

"What happened?"

His voice was desperate. "The very thing José de Carlon wrote about and warned about. Whatever it is, she has it—the curse of Toco-Rey!"

FIVE

Armond Basehart and his three men were suddenly startled by faraway, echoing screams coming out of the pit like anguished screams from hell. Tomás, Juan, and Carlos crouched, gripping their rifles, their eyes white and wide with terror in the dark of the jungle.

Even scientific-minded Dr. Basehart was unnerved by the sound. "It's—I think it's the girl."

Tomás nodded, his face etched with fear. "This is not good, señor. It's—"

The sound was getting closer, louder, wilder. They could hear running footsteps, the other Coopers shouting, the girl screaming. All the voices echoed from far below like ghosts in a deep, forbidden crypt.

Dr. Basehart leaned over the wall and shined his light into the pit. "One of you had better get down there and see what happened." He looked at his men. "It could be—AAUUGH!"

Something grabbed his arm, then the edge of his coat, then clawed and climbed over him like a wild cat, knocking him to the ground. Juan and Carlos cursed in Spanish, unable to believe their eyes.

"Grab her!" Tomás yelled. "Señorita, stop!"

Juan dropped his rifle to free his hands. She was coming right at him, her eyes wild, her teeth bared, her breath huffing.

He tried to stop her, plead with her. He grabbed hold of her. "Señorita, please—"

She threw him off as if he weighed nothing, and he tumbled head over heels into the brush. Without looking back, she ran headlong into the jungle. They could hear her crashing through the thick growth into the dark night, getting farther and farther away. She screamed again.

And then they heard another scream—*the* other scream, from somewhere in the ruins. It seemed to be answering her.

"Basehart!" came Dr. Cooper's voice from below.

Dr. Basehart and his men dove at the rope and pulled Dr. Cooper from the pit.

"Where's my daughter?" Jacob Cooper demanded, scrambling over the wall.

"She . . ." Dr. Basehart fumbled to answer, still in shock.

"*Where is she?*" he yelled.

Dr. Basehart's voice trembled. "She ran into the jungle. We couldn't stop her. She was mad, out of her mind!"

"Get my son out of there!"

They quickly pulled Jay out of the pit.

Dr. Cooper was seething. "So the green slugs are harmless, eh?" He grabbed Tomás by the collar.

"You call *that* harmless? My daughter is a raving animal!"

Dr. Basehart intervened, pulling Jacob Cooper away from Tomás. "Dr. Cooper, we are just as surprised as you! We had no idea—"

They heard another scream. It was Lila.

"Come on," said Dr. Cooper, leading the way into the jungle, "we'll talk later."

Tomás cautioned, "It is dangerous! There are snakes, carvies, maybe Kachakas!"

"Come on!"

They pushed into the jungle, trying their best to follow Lila's trail. Dr. Cooper kept probing the thick growth with his flashlight, finding broken branches, trampled leaves and vines, footprints in the soft earth. Her speed and agility through this tangled mess was uncanny. Not only was she out of her mind, but a massive adrenaline rush also gave her super strength. Sometimes it seemed she had bounded over the top of everything.

"The curse of Toco-Rey," Dr. Cooper muttered bitterly, groping about, slashing with his machete. "Toxic slime! That's all José de Carlon encountered. That's all it ever was. I shouldn't have believed Tomás. I should have gotten Lila out of here right away and put her in a hospital!"

Dr. Basehart tried to defend himself. "Dr. Cooper, we can't be sure what caused—"

"Then find out!" Dr. Cooper snapped back. "You're the scientist, the biologist with the lab. Find out what the stuff is and how we can undo whatever it's doing!"

"My primary purpose here is not biological research, Doctor!" Basehart objected loudly. "I'm here to find the treasure of Kachi-Tochetin—and so are you, I might add!"

Dr. Cooper spun around, eyes blazing, clenching a fist, ready to strike. He quickly controlled himself but struck hard with his words. "Put your greed on hold, Dr. Basehart, until we find my daughter!" He turned and continued pushing through the brush.

Armond Basehart followed, clearly offended. "I beg your pardon!"

"You heard me! You and your boss can just—"

They burst into the clear.

Juan screamed. The others froze, guns in hand.

They were standing before the crumbling stone wall of what had been an Oltecan dwelling. On the ground at the base of the wall, a human-shaped mass of squirming, slimy blobs boiled, crawled, hissed, and squeaked.

For a moment, no one moved. No one could think of what to do.

Tomás came up behind Dr. Cooper and whispered in his ear. "They are turning from yellow to green," Tomás noted. "They may be more timid now."

Dr. Cooper approached cautiously, machete and spray bottle ready to take on any carvy that came near him. Some of the slimy creatures began to notice him and half-fly, half-hop away.

So suddenly that he startled the others, Jacob Cooper yelled and flashed his machete back and forth, causing a commotion that sent the carvies fluttering into the trees and ruins like a flock of frightened birds.

"Oh no . . ." said Dr. Basehart as he looked, horrified, at what remained on the ground.

Tomás took one look and then crossed himself.

Jacob Cooper approached cautiously, shining his flashlight on the remains of a person, now nothing more than a skeleton covered with green slime, propped against the wall. "It's Brad Frederick, one of the Cory party."

The others moved closer in shock and amazement, flashlights illuminating the dead, grinning skeleton before them.

"How can you tell?" Dr. Basehart asked.

"Remember the video?" Dr. Cooper responded, shining his light in the skeleton's face. "That big, white grin is unmistakable."

"No one touch it," Dr. Basehart cautioned as he knelt beside the skeleton to scrape off a sample of the green slime with a stick. "I'll take this sample back to the lab and see if I can match it with the slime we took from Lila earlier today." He carefully folded the stick in his handkerchief and placed it in a vest pocket. "But now it all makes perfect sense, doesn't it?"

"Does it?" Dr. Cooper asked.

Dr. Basehart looked up at the group. "The slug toxin. The Kachakas use it to tip their darts. We found darts at the Corys' camp, so we know the Kachakas must have attacked them. This man, Brad Frederick, must have been hit with a poison dart, and he contracted the same symptoms as your daughter: madness and extreme paranoia, followed eventually by paralysis and death. He fled the scene of the attack, wandered among these ruins, and finally succumbed here. The carvies are the jungle's housekeepers. They have, uh, cleaned up the remains in their own way." Now he directed his words to Tomás, Juan, and Carlos. "So this 'curse' you've been so afraid of is nothing more than the toxin the carvies produce in their slime. Nature itself has found a way to guard the treasure of Kachi-Tochetin: poisonous slugs."

Tomás tried to argue. "But Señor Basehart, Juan and Carlos and I have all touched the green slime before. We have handled the green slugs. We have never gone crazy. The slime does not hurt us."

Basehart thought that over. "Your ancestors have probably developed an immunity over the generations. The slime, regardless of its color, could produce a very different reaction in foreigners." He looked at the Coopers. "Which could be why Kachi-Tochetin found it so appropriate."

Jay had been pondering something for several moments, and now he finally got the chance to ask, "But Dr. Basehart, if this is Brad Frederick, then who's buried in the grave back at the Corys' camp?"

For just an instant, Dr. Basehart seemed stumped by the question. "I forgot. There were *four* in the Cory party. We buried the three we found in the camp. This one, Mr. Frederick, met his terrible fate here in the ruins." Dr. Basehart rose to his feet ceremoniously. "But now he, too, will be buried in a proper grave. We will see to that."

Jacob Cooper was quite edgy. "But first we have to find Lila, before she ends up"—he shot a glance toward the skeleton at their feet—"like this."

Jay swallowed. The thought was too horrible to imagine. "Man, let's go."

"Tomás and Juan will help you search," said Dr. Basehart, not even looking at his men to see if they approved of their assignment. "Carlos will accompany me back to the lab. I'm going to analyze this sample to see if I can isolate the toxin. We'll have to hope I can find an antidote in time."

"We'll find Lila," said Dr. Cooper with grave determination, "and we'll bring her to you."

They were startled by another long, mournful wail deep within the ruins.

"That's Lila," said Jay excitedly. "She's not too far away."

"Good luck," said Dr. Basehart, heading back toward the compound.

Dr. Cooper instructed Tomás, "You and Juan circle that way; Jay and I will go this way. We'll try to keep Lila between us until we can narrow down her location."

They split up and headed into the jungle, moving slowly, cautiously. They kept an eye open for snakes and yellow carvies while keeping an ear open for any other sounds from Lila.

After they had gone some distance, Dr. Cooper stopped and motioned for Jay to hold up. They listened a moment. There was no sound.

And then there was. Another long, mournful wail.

"Dad," Jay whispered in concern, "that wasn't Lila."

Jacob Cooper nodded, then whispered, "Which means Armond Basehart has some explaining to do."

"What do you mean?"

"He worked with the Cory party until they were killed. He had the video, he knew them by name, and now he's asking us to believe that he buried three of them and forgot about the other two."

"Two?"

"Brad Frederick . . . and now this other scream we've been hearing." Dr. Cooper listened a moment, but there was no other sound. "It's a human being in anguish, just like Lila. If you ask me, I think it's another one of the Cory party."

Jay wrinkled his nose. "So there were *five* people on the Cory team?"

"We don't know. But I'm bothered that Dr. Basehart doesn't seem to remember."

Jay asked, "If two of them went crazy like Lila, why would he try to hide that from us?"

Dr. Cooper sighed with disgust. "Greed. He's so intent on finding the treasure that he doesn't want us concerning ourselves with the Corys."

Jay thought it over, then nodded. "Yeah. If we thought the Corys were still alive, we'd be trying to help them instead of searching for the treasure."

"Exactly. I don't think a man like Armond Basehart has time for such moral considerations. And I don't think he was planning on us finding that skeleton—or hearing these screams."

"So what really happened? Were the Corys

attacked by the Kachakas or did they go crazy from contact with slug slime, or was it both, or what?"

"I think Armond Basehart knows but isn't telling. And now I'm wondering if he really has claustrophobia. It could be he's—"

A scream, then snarling and more screaming and thrashing in the brush: It was close by.

Dr. Cooper and Jay dove into the brush, shouldering their way through it, pushing, plowing, clawing ahead. It sounded like a chase out there: a victim fleeing, a predator hunting. They could envision the worst.

They broke out of the brush and into a clearing. They'd found more ruins—more gray, crumbling stone jutting up through the thick undergrowth. They shined their lights back and forth, the beams searching, searching. Someone was running, screaming, struggling on the other side of that crumbling wall. They caught sight of a droopy, billed cap.

"It's Lila!" Dr. Cooper exclaimed, running toward the ruin, his gun in his hand and Jay right alongside.

They leaped to the top of the wall. It was an old dwelling, four walls with no roof. Over in the corner, amid vines and plants, their light beams caught a young girl cowering in terror, her body curled up, her arms over her head.

"Lila!" her dad hollered, jumping down from the wall and running toward her.

Still atop the wall, Jay saw the bushes moving. Something was heading in Dr. Cooper's direction.

"Dad!"

Dr. Cooper heard the warning, felt a commotion to his left, and looked just in time to see—teeth! flashing eyes! a powerful fist!

He deflected the blow, ducked another one, then crouched down and used a judo move the third time to throw the creature into the bushes. It thrashed about, righting itself, leaping to its feet. It came at him again.

He had dropped his gun and the flashlight. No time to look for them.

The thing took a powerful leap through the air, arms outstretched, fingers like claws, a scream in its throat. Dr. Cooper ducked, deflected the weight, threw it off. Once again, it tumbled into the bushes.

No way to overpower it, Dr. Cooper thought. *I can only deflect it, but for how long?* He saw a metallic gleam amid the vines several feet away. He started to reach for it.

OOF! The blow knocked him sideways into green vines and crackling branches. He rolled onto his back and saw a face coming out of the dark. It was green, raging, other-worldly, drooling, full of murder.

The creature leaped. Jacob Cooper planted a foot in its belly and kicked it over his head and into the bushes again.

Now for that gun! He groped for it, searched for it. *BOOM!*

Jay had found it and fired a round into the air.

The thing let out a cry of alarm and seemed to hesitate.

"Go on!" Jay hollered, shooting into the air again. "Get out of here!"

It turned and fled, thrashing through the brush.

Dr. Cooper got to his feet.

"Dad!" Jay screamed, "Look out!"

Dr. Cooper spun around, saw it coming, ducked.

A poison dart thunked into a branch right next to his head.

Poof! A puff of air. A second dart zipped past Jay's ear.

The Coopers dropped to the ground, scurried, crawled, then peered through the leaves and branches. Dr. Cooper found his flashlight.

The light beam fell on a small hand clutching a short length of bamboo cane, aiming it.

Poof! Another dart zinged through the leaves and branches only inches from Dr. Cooper's head.

"Don't shoot!" he called. "We're friends!"

They heard a frightened gasp. No more darts came their way.

"Hello?" Jacob Cooper called again. "Can you see us? We're friends. We won't hurt you."

They poked their heads up and waved their hands so they could be clearly seen.

A dark-skinned, native girl looked back at them, a blowgun in her hand. Her face was full of fear. But when she saw them, she seemed to relax.

Then she let out a sigh and slumped to the ground in a faint.

They rushed forward to help her, cradling her head, feeling for a pulse. Her heartbeat was strong and she was breathing okay.

"Poor thing," said Dr. Cooper. "She must have been terrified." He picked up her blowgun and slipped it into his shirt pocket, then he used his flashlight to illumine the olive-skinned face and long, jet black hair. She was young, beautiful, close to Lila's age and stature.

"She's a native," Dr. Cooper observed. "Probably a Kachaka."

Jay was dismayed. "How'd she get Lila's hat?"

"She may have found it . . . or she could have encountered Lila." He gently stroked her forehead and spoke to her. "Hello, little girl. Come on, wake up."

A glow fell upon the girl's face and the stones of the old wall. There was a sound behind them.

As they turned, they saw torches coming over the wall and the dimly lit outlines of several men— *big* men—in loose clothing, some bare-chested. Some wore straw hats. They were carrying knives, rifles, clubs. A voice jabbered at them in an unknown language. More torches appeared. The light washed over the area.

A man approached them ahead of the others, his intense, lined face clear in the light of the torches. He was a native. Wearing pants and a ragged shirt topped by a tattered straw hat, he also carried an old rifle. When he saw them with the pitiful, unconscious girl, his eyes filled with horror and then rage. He screamed at them, aiming his rifle.

They let go of the girl and raised their hands.

The man screamed orders to his men, who immediately pushed through the brush toward them, brandishing their weapons. Two grabbed Jacob Cooper, putting a knife to his throat. Two more grabbed Jay and held him, taking away his father's gun. Two others gently picked up the girl and carried her aside. One more helped himself to the Coopers' flashlights.

Dr. Cooper spoke, though he was careful not to move or give his captors any reason to use the knife. "We were trying to help her. She was being attacked."

The man seemed amused. "You like to make up stories?"

Here was a little hope. "You know English?"

The man cocked his head and smirked as if he'd heard a dumb question. "I pick up a little here and there. Yours sounds very good."

"Sir, we *rescued* your daughter. She was being attacked—"

"By *you!*" the man hollered, gesturing with the barrel of the rifle. "You cannot fool me! You are mukai-tochetin!" His eyes darted about the ruins for an instant as if looking for hidden dangers. "You are everywhere! You want to scare us and kill us. Why? We are Kachakas! We did not violate the tomb!"

Uh-oh. This could be serious. "You are Kachakas?"

"You know that. Mukai-tochetin know everything. You know I am the chief, and you know the girl is my daughter." He raised his rifle and appeared to be seriously considering pulling the trigger. "And that is why you tried to kill her, yes? To hurt *me!*"

"Sir . . . I am Dr. Jacob Cooper from America, and this is my son, Jay—"

The chief aimed the rifle directly into Dr. Cooper's face. Dr. Cooper could see right along the barrel into his eye. "No more lies! You only want to scare us, to kill us, to kill my daughter and hurt me!" He pulled back the hammer. "But I think I hurt you first!"

SIX

Another man shouted at the chief and then spoke hurriedly, as if trying to reason with him. It must have been a good argument—the chief uncocked his rifle and lowered it. The two talked a moment, throwing suggestions and counter-suggestions back and forth and pointing at the Coopers.

Finally, the chief gave in and spoke in English. "We take you to our village." He jerked his thumb toward the man who argued with him. "Manito says if you are really mukai-tochetin, it will do no good to shoot you. But he thinks you are not mukai-tochetin. He thinks maybe you are just stupid Americans. We find out."

With some not-so-gentle prodding from their well-armed captors, Jay and Dr. Cooper started walking through the ruins toward the unexplored jungle on the other side.

Jacob Cooper's anxiety was obvious as he told Jay, "We sure don't need this right now. Lila's still out there, probably dying."

"So how do we get out of it?" Jay responded.

The chief was walking just ahead of them. Dr. Cooper called to him, "Uh, Chief . . ."

"Chief Yoaxa," the chief informed him.

"Thank you. Chief Yoaxa. Listen, my daughter is lost somewhere in these ruins and in great danger. We were trying to find her when we found your daughter instead. Your daughter was being attacked by a, uh, a wild man. I don't know how else to describe it."

The chief gave Dr. Cooper a good, long look and then smiled craftily. "Oh yes. A wild man. A mukai-tochetin!"

"Mukai-tochetin." Jay was getting sick of the word. "What is that, anyway?"

The chief grinned as if being joked with. "You mukai-tochetin are very tricky. You try to test me, yes? But I know. When the great king Kachi-Tochetin was buried in his tomb, his best warriors were buried with him so their spirits would guard his treasure. You see? I know what you are." His eyes narrowed with bitter anger. "But why are you out of your tomb? Why do you bother us? We do not like to be scared and screamed at and attacked! We have never bothered your treasure! We have not even seen it! We do not deserve the curse!" He gestured with his rifle, making his message clear. "You should go back to sleep in your tomb. Leave the living world to us!"

Dr. Cooper and Jay exchanged a glance. This was the Kachaka explanation for the toxin-induced madness!

"Chief Yoaxa, listen," said Dr. Cooper. "I have

good news for you. These people who are wandering about in the ruins are not the warriors of Kachi-Tochetin, not at all. They are explorers from America who have . . . well, they're sick and dying. They're out of their minds because—"

"Because they are ghosts." The chief pointed his finger right in their faces. "And you are ghosts, dead warriors, just like them!"

"Chief, we are not dead warriors."

The chief was getting impatient. "You attacked my daughter!"

Dr. Cooper was also getting impatient. "We did *not* attack your daughter! We saved your daughter from—well, from one of the sick Americans. He almost killed us and your daughter shot poison darts at us . . . If anything, we deserve your thanks!"

The chief got angry when he heard that. "See? You lie! Kachaka children do not shoot poison darts. We forbid it!"

"Well, that may be true but—"

The chief held up his hand. "No more talking! When we get to the village, we find out."

They continued along a well-beaten path through the jungle. Eventually they reached a small village where at least two hundred men, women, and children waited anxiously for the return of their chief and his men. The village was an odd mixture of old and new, of civilized and savage. Grass huts stood alongside crude, wood-framed dwellings; there were campfires but also cookstoves. Both torches and oil lanterns lit the narrow corridor between the dwellings. A few folks didn't seem to mind wearing little or nothing while they worked, yet most of the people were fully dressed in white garments, some skillfully embroidered.

As for the Kachakas' choice of weapons, almost every warrior carried a blowgun on his belt, but many also carried rifles, pistols, and knives.

Some of the women in the village looked especially anxious, as if they had been dreading this moment. When they saw the limp body of the girl being carried by the two men, they threw up their hands and wailed in fear and anguish. With tears and rapid-fire babblings of concern, they gently took her from her two carriers and bore her into the nearest wooden shack where they laid her on a cot.

The chief stopped just outside the door of the crude dwelling, watching the women work to revive the girl, then turned to the Coopers. "See the pain you have brought? She has been missing since early evening, and we looked for her until it was a long time dark. We told all the children, 'Don't go into the ruins, there are mukai-tochetin there.'" The chief shook his head as he peered through the doorway at his unconscious daughter. "I think that is why she went. She has always wanted to see one." He looked at Dr. Cooper. "Well . . . now she has."

Jacob Cooper couldn't help sighing in frustration. "Chief Yoaxa—"

"Follow me," the chief said, waving his hand and leading the way.

The men holding the Coopers prodded them forward through the village, past the humble grass huts, clapboard shacks, firepits, and milling, curious people.

Jay noticed a man wearing a strange, disk-shaped charm around his neck. Then he saw another one. Then Dr. Cooper spotted two more.

The Kachakas were wearing the dried, stretched skins of *caracoles volantes* as jewelry!

"Carvies!" Jay exclaimed.

That made the chief turn his head. "You should be happy. We wear carvies to please you, but . . . I guess not today."

Jay tried to win a few points. "Oh, but we're *very* pleased."

The chief brightened. "Then you *are* mukai-tochetin!"

Jay made a sour face, mentally kicking himself.

Jacob Cooper coaxed some information. "I understand they're poisonous."

Chief Yoaxa enjoyed answering that question. "Oh, yes, they are poisonous. They will kill you just by touching you. Unless . . ."

"Unless what?"

"Unless you catch them in the morning. Then they don't hurt you. We play with them, we cook them and eat them, and there is no trouble."

Dr. Cooper nodded. "Yes. We've been told that."

They came to the end of the village and turned a corner. Directly ahead of them was what looked like a row of rabbit hutches and a large chicken pen, all made from poles and wire mesh.

The Coopers stopped short at the sight of the cages. The men behind them poked them forward.

73

The rabbit hutches and the chicken pen were full of carvies—yellow, angry carvies. The slugs came to life the moment the group approached. Flapping about in the cages, hissing, and chirping, they flitted from wall to wall, their little black eyes devilish and threatening.

"These carvies, they are special," said the chief. "We caught them in the morning, so it was easy, but then we kept them in these cages until night. You do that and they get dangerous. Just watch."

The chief pulled a small, sharpened dart from a quiver on his belt. Sticking it through the wire mesh, he rubbed its tip against a yellow carvy's slimy back. When he withdrew it, the tip of the dart glistened.

Dr. Cooper eyed the dart carefully. "So this is the poison dart of the Kachakas?"

The chief held it up proudly. "Yes. We make them ourselves! Now watch."

He skillfully inserted the dart into the blowgun that hung over his shoulder, then looked for a target. Some pigs were grunting and rooting in the grass nearby. He put the blowgun to his mouth, gave it a strong blast of air, and the dart shot like an arrow, sticking a pig in the flank.

The pig did more than squeal; it shrieked, twirled, grunted, scurried in a little circle, and then flopped to the ground, legs twitching. In only seconds, it was dead.

The chief grinned. "It works quick, you see? It can kill you. Unless . . ."

"Unless what?" Dr. Cooper asked.

The chief smiled jubilantly. "Unless you are dead already."

Dr. Cooper's heart sank. "Oh. Of course."

"We have a legend: The carvies belong to the mukai-tochetin. Together, they guard the treasure. If you are one of Kachi-Tochetin's warriors, the yellow carvies will not hurt you."

Dr. Cooper could see where this was leading and did not like it one bit. "But as I've been trying to tell you, we're not ghosts, or warriors, or anything else. We're living, breathing American explorers."

The chief shrugged again. "We'll find out. If you are dead already, the yellow carvies won't hurt you—so we'll take you back to Toco-Rey and bury you where you belong. If you are just stupid Americans, the carvies will kill you—and I'll admit I was wrong."

Suddenly, the chief's men had a much firmer grip on Jay and his father. They meant business.

Dr. Cooper tried to remain calm and rational, though being only a few feet from a swarm of yellow carvies made that difficult. "Chief, does it make any sense for the warriors of Kachi-Tochetin to have white skin, speak English, and dress like Americans?"

This time the chief sighed. "The warriors we have seen in the ruins have green skin, they don't dress much at all, and they don't speak English. They yell and scream."

Jay objected, "So what about us? We have white skin, we're dressed, and we speak English! I mean, *come on* . . . !"

The chief thought about that for a moment, but he was a stubborn man, and all his men were watching. "Like I say, mukai-tochetin are very tricky."

"Chief Yoaxa!" Dr. Cooper talked slowly and

deliberately, trying to spell it out. "Listen to me: Those green, screaming warriors are Americans who have come in contact with the slime from the carvies. The slime has made them crazy, and it's killing them. We've seen it. There's a dead man in the ruins right now—and my daughter is still out there, poisoned, mad, and dying. Instead of killing us, why don't you help us?"

The chief's face lit up and he pointed his finger in Jacob Cooper's face. "Ah! You see? You think you can fool me. Carvies don't make you crazy. They kill you."

"But—"

"Listen, I'm giving you a good deal. You should take it and be glad."

Dr. Cooper looked at the chief, then at Jay, then back at the chief, thinking it all over. Then, strangely, he relaxed and nodded. "All right. You've convinced me. We'll take your test."

Jay did *not* agree. "Dad! You can't let them do this!"

Dr. Cooper straightened his spine, drew a deep breath, and put a consoling hand on his son's shoulder. "Son, there comes a time when we simply have to face our destiny like real men."

"We do?" Jay looked up and read a message in his father's eyes. "Oh. Uh, yeah, you're right, Dad. Yeah. Like real men."

The carvies in the big cage were drooling and hissing at Dr. Cooper even as he looked at the men guarding him. "Gentlemen, I agree to the chief's offer. Shall we proceed?"

Dr. Cooper no longer resisted them, but stood there relaxed, willing and ready. He could tell they were impressed by that; their grip on him eased up a bit. He stepped forward to the cage door. "I only hope that once I'm dead, you'll go out and find my daughter." He looked at the chief. "And I believe your daughter will be all right. I think she only fainted." He gently raised his left arm to remove his hat. The man holding him allowed him to do so. "Let justice be done."

He turned to hand his hat to the men behind him. They were impressed by his gentle compliance; they actually released him.

The man who took his hat was the first to see a huge fist, and then stars. The other man caught Jacob Cooper's left hook a fraction of a second later, and then he saw only grass.

Jay was expecting his father's move and made some quick moves himself, first planting his foot behind the man on his right to trip him. Then he spun and planted his foot in the groin of the other man to give him something to think about.

"Run!" his father shouted, taking on three Kachakas while ten more closed in on him.

With his father holding back the Kachakas, Jay turned and ran like the wind. Out of the village and into the cover of the jungle, he had little idea of which way to go except toward the ruins. Tomás and Juan had to be out there somewhere. They had rifles and could help, if only he could find them! He could hear the struggle going on back in the village: the shouts, the blows. Then his father yelled one more time, "Run, Jay, run!" Jay tried to hold back his tears. In the dark of the jungle, he was nearly blind as it was.

By now, Dr. Cooper could see nothing but Kachaka faces, bodies, and arms. He was floating in a mob of angry, shouting natives. They held his arms, his legs, his hair. He couldn't struggle or trip or punch or even move. It was over. From somewhere he could hear the chief yell an order. The mob started moving as one man toward the cage.

Dear Lord, he prayed. *Just let Jay make it out of here. And remember Lila, wherever she is.*

He could hear someone fumbling with the cage door. The carvies were going absolutely wild.

And then the crowd fell quiet. He could hear the chief's voice now, not yelling but talking to someone. The someone was a woman.

The voice of a young girl joined them. He couldn't understand the language, but she was speaking clearly. The chief's daughter? It had to be!

The Kachakas carrying Dr. Cooper eased their grip and set him on the ground. Many of them actually let go and backed off. When enough of their bodies were out of the way, he could finally see that the chief was talking to a lovely woman, most likely his wife, and . . . oh, praise God! The chief's daughter! She was still wearing Lila's droopy, billed cap, and she pointed at Dr. Cooper, rapidly explaining something to her father. He kept objecting and trying to argue, but apparently she would not change her opinion.

Finally the chief straightened up, looked at Dr. Cooper with disappointment and embarrassment, and gave his men an order. They all let go of Dr. Cooper and gave him some space. One even returned his hat.

"My daughter says you did not attack her," the chief admitted. "She says you . . ." He really hated to say it. "She says you saved her from a mukai-tochetin."

Dr. Cooper exhaled a sigh of relief. His shoulders relaxed as he returned the girl's gaze. Her eyes were clear and beautiful. He could tell her mind and memory were intact.

She must have learned her heavily accented English from her father. "Gracias, Señor American, for saving my life."

Dr. Cooper removed his newly returned hat to show his respect and gratitude. "You're most welcome. And thank you for saving mine." He stole a quick glance at the chief to make sure he was correct in saying that.

The chief was reluctant, but finally nodded yes. "You are not mukai-tochetin. One mukai-tochetin would not fight another." He put his hand on his daughter's shoulder. "This is María. María, this is . . ."

"Dr. Jacob Cooper." He took just a few steps toward the girl, reached into his shirt pocket, and brought out her small blowgun. "I believe this belongs to you."

She took one look at it and shook her head. "Oh no," she said emphatically. "That is not mine."

Hmm. Interesting. Dr. Cooper played along.

"Oh. Well, it must belong to one of the men here."
He tossed it to the nearest Kachaka warrior, who
looked it over, shook his head, and then passed it to
the next. It began circulating among the men in
search of an owner. "But please, can you tell me if
you've seen my daughter? She's about your age and
height, with fair skin and long, blond hair. She's lost
somewhere in the ruins."

The girl's eyes betrayed some kind of knowledge,
but she was hesitant to speak.

Jacob Cooper prompted, "That is my daughter
Lila's hat. Where did you find it?"

She still hesitated until her mother bent and
spoke some quiet but firm words in her ear. Then
she admitted, "I got this hat from a mukai-
tochetin."

That brought a gasp from some of the women
standing nearby and alarmed looks from all of the
men, including her father.

"Tell him the rest," her father ordered. "Tell *us!*"

"She was a girl, like me. Her face . . ." She
touched her cheek as she spoke it. "Her face was
green, like a lizard."

The Kachakas muttered to each other, exchang-
ing looks of alarm.

"Did she attack you?" the chief asked with a suspicious, sideways glance at Dr. Cooper.

The girl hesitated, then answered timidly. "Sí. She
. . . she jumped out of the bushes and screamed at
me. She was like a crazy person. . . ."

"*She* was a mukai-tochetin!" the chief proclaimed
as if trying to regain his pride. "What did you do?"

80

"I ran."

"You ran away?"

"Sí."

The chief patted her shoulder. "Ah. That was good."

Dr. Cooper asked, "Then . . . how did you get her hat?"

The girl thought a moment, then replied. "I found her later. She was lying on the ground. And I took her hat."

Dr. Cooper leaned forward. "Lying on the ground? Why? Was something wrong with her?"

The girl looked from Dr. Cooper to the Kachaka men and women to her father and mother, and then at Dr. Cooper again. "She is dead."

SEVEN

Jacob Cooper could not give up hope. "Can you take me to her? Can you show me where she is?"

She looked to her father. He nodded that it would be okay. "Sí, señor."

"We need to go," said Dr. Cooper. "Right now. Jay's out there somewhere, too."

Chief Yoaxa chose four of his toughest men to go with them. Then quickly, to get it over with, he handed Dr. Cooper his gun and two flashlights. "You will want these in the ruins."

María headed through the village while Dr. Cooper, her father, and four burly Kachakas followed. They took the main trail into the jungle, carrying torches and lanterns, guns and knives, as well as Kachaka blowguns with plenty of darts.

Jay thought he knew where he was when he came to an old stone wall, but it was so covered with jungle growth that he totally lost his bearings as he tried to explore around it. Finally, breaking out from under the thick jungle canopy, he saw stars overhead and determined which direction was north. He'd gotten turned around, all right. Doing a complete about-face, he headed the other direction, south, hoping to encounter the Pyramid of the Sun or any other familiar landmark. He had to get back to the compound and find help.

He was thinking of his father and sister, and how little time there was. Hope was hard to hang onto, but he tried.

Lila Cooper was not dead. She was dazed, half-conscious, half-dreaming, lying amid vines and rubble at the base of a lone, basalt pillar that had held up a roof centuries ago. She was still dressed in the extra clothes she'd put on to protect herself from slug slime, and she was feeling hot, sweaty, tired, and achy.

But she didn't want to wake up. Somehow she knew there was a very spooky world beyond her closed eyelids. It was better to hide inside her dazed mind where the world was all laughing, dancing colors; the ground was still moving like a carnival ride; and no bogeymen could get her.

"Señorita?" came a voice from somewhere.

Who was that, the bogeyman? Go away. I don't believe in you.

"Señorita?" came the voice again, and then it started talking in hushed tones with another voice. It was all Spanish; she couldn't understand much of it.

She could sense a light shining on her eyelids. It made her squint.

"Aha!" said the voice. "Está viva!"

She raised her hand to her face and then opened her eyes just a crack. There were lights out there, shining in her face.

"Señorita Cooper, it is us, Juan and Tomás. Are you all right?"

Tomás. It took her a moment to remember who he was. She opened her eyes completely and could make out two men kneeling beside her with their flashlights.

"Tomás?" she heard herself saying.

"Sí, señorita. It is a good thing we found you. How are you feeling?"

"Hot."

She sat up and removed her gloves and extra shirt. When she raised her hand to wipe the hair from her eyes, she saw something peculiar. She looked at her hand again, then leaned forward to view it in the beam of Tomás's flashlight. "What happened?"

"We think it was the carvy slime, señorita. It made you loco . . . crazy . . . and it made you look a little green." Tomás chuckled, and so did Juan.

"A little . . . ," Her hand looked *very* green to her.

Juan shined his flashlight on her hands and face and made some comments.

Tomás agreed and told Lila, "It was much worse, but you seem to be getting better now. Can you stand up? We will take you back to the compound."

She tried to get her feet under her. With Tomás's strong arms to help, she finally stood up. "Ouch!" Her hand went to her leg. "My leg hurts."

"Would you like me to carry you?"

She tried to walk. After a few shaky steps, it came a little more easily. "Where are my father and brother?"

"They are out looking for you. We'll get you safely back, and then we'll find them, don't worry."

María knew the ruins well, even in the dark. She led her father, the Kachaka warriors, and Dr. Cooper directly through the jungle to an old basalt pillar that had once supported a roof.

There María was disturbed to find Lila gone. "She . . . was lying right here! I saw her! I took her hat!"

Chief Yoaxa puffed up his chest and crossed his arms. "Ha! She is a mukai-tochetin! She cannot die. She will haunt these ruins forever!"

Dr. Cooper looked at the area carefully. It was matted down as if someone had been lying there. "María . . . how long ago was that?"

"It was before the mukai-tochetin chased me."

"The wild, green man?"

"Yes. He came from over there." She pointed toward a spooky looking, pillared temple just barely visible in the dark.

"He chased me, but you came to help me—"

"Yes, he came to help you, like the great hero!" Chief Yoaxa cut in, tired of hearing that story. He glared at Dr. Cooper. "Manito thinks you are okay, and María thinks you are okay, but I think you are a mukai-tochetin, like your daughter. You have bewitched María to lie!"

Dr. Cooper had no time to argue further. "Lila's still out here somewhere, and we have to find her—"

The scream. It came from *out there* somewhere, out in the limitless dark jungle.

Chief Yoaxa and his men were clearly frightened. "We must get back to our village now."

"No, wait," Dr. Cooper objected. "I need your help."

The Chief gathered his daughter close to him. "You do not need *our* help, Dr. Cooper!" He looked into the dead ruins and ink-black jungle. "You have the mukai-tochetin! They are your friends, yes? Your daughter is one of them. I think you are too. Maybe this is all a trap!"

Chief Yoaxa's men started to buy into his argument. They began to edge away.

"Wait!" said Dr. Cooper. "You know these ruins. You can help me search!"

The scream echoed through the ruins again, and they all turned tail and ran, leaving Jacob Cooper alone amid the aging stones, the bottomless shadows, the eerie sounds.

Dr. Armond Basehart held the syringe up to the light. It was full of red blood, a good sample. He was satisfied.

Lila had shed the extra clothes she'd worn into the pit and sat comfortably on a couch in his lab, pressing a cotton ball to the puncture in her arm. "What about my father and brother?"

"Tomás, Juan, and Carlos are out searching for them right now," he answered, preparing to distribute her blood into several small test tubes. "They'll be all right. But we have to do all we can to find out what happened to you before the symptoms are totally gone."

She looked at her arms. They still had a greenish cast but were steadily returning to their natural pink. "It's going away pretty fast."

He leaned over her with a cotton swab. "Lean back."

She looked up. "Huh?"

He forced her head back with his hand on her forehead, a touch she did not appreciate, and took a smear sample from her nostrils.

"What's that for?" she asked, wrinkling her nose to relieve the tickle of the swab.

Instead of answering her question, he asked, "Did you see or touch anything unusual before you fell into the pit the first time?"

She thought it over and then shook her head. "All I remember is falling into all those slugs and getting slime all over me."

"Anything afterward?"

"The pit," she answered. "The pit was weird."

"Mm-hm."

Dr. Basehart rolled the cotton swab along a microscope slide. Then he put the slide under his microscope and slowly turned the focus knob.

From the look on his face, Lila could see he'd found something interesting. "What do you see?"

He ignored her question.

She didn't mind asking again. "What's . . . uh, what are you looking at?"

He gave an exasperated sigh like he didn't want

to answer her question, but then he turned and smiled at her. The smile looked a little phony. "Oh, pollen, dust . . . even a tiny bug!"

In her *nose*? "Oh, yuk!"

He just laughed.

"Can I see?"

He waved her off. "No, not now. I have too many things to process here."

His tone actually sounded a little harsh. She didn't argue with him. She was too tired and she didn't want to aggravate him. Besides, a burning itch on her lower leg was screaming for attention. She pulled her sock down to scratch it and found a welt. "Hey, Dr. Basehart. The green's going away faster around this insect bite. Does that mean anything?"

He didn't seem to mind that question. He came over immediately to take a closer look. The welt seemed to fascinate him for a moment, but then he just shook his head. "Mm, no, I think that's coincidental."

"Sure hurts," she complained.

"Well, the insects around here can bite pretty hard!" He patted her on the shoulder. "I think I'm all through with you for now. Why don't you go to your trailer and see if you can sleep?"

He went back to the counter and started arranging various samples in a neat row. Lila recognized some of them: the slime he'd wiped from her after she fell in the pit; the blood he'd drawn from her arm; the smear he'd just taken from her nose. He wouldn't say anything, but he had figured something out, she could tell.

And he was excited about whatever it was.

At last! Jay came to the huge pillars that formed the gate to the city. A spare flashlight would have helped immensely, but he had no time for a side trip to the burial temple to get his backpack. Running through the gates, he prayed the Lord would help him find the safe route through the treacherous swamp. He couldn't wait to get back to the compound.

Jay didn't know that his father was only a mile or so behind him, rushing desperately to catch up. Dr. Cooper could not call out for his son for fear he'd attract the mad man again. All he could do was hurry along, picking his way through the jungle. He located the Pyramid of the Sun, the Avenue of the Dead, and the Pyramid of the Moon. He'd been putting pieces together in his mind and was certain there were no friends waiting for Jay at the compound— only a cunning enemy.

Lila decided she'd follow Dr. Basehart's suggestion and go back to the guest trailer to get some sleep. Soon she would see her father and brother again. After they all rested up, they could get back to finding the treasure with no more interruptions.

I've caused everyone enough trouble, she thought.

But she had another reason for wanting to get out of Armond Basehart's lab trailer, and that was Dr. Basehart. Something about him gave her the creeps, and she didn't need any more needle pokes in her arm or cotton swabs up her nose—not from him, anyway.

She stepped outside, closed the door behind her, and paused to listen to the jungle sounds on the still night air. When would this long night be over, anyway? She wasn't sure what time it was, but it had to be getting close to morning by now.

Hmm. Was that another vehicle parked just behind the rig the Coopers had brought? Had someone new come to the compound? As far as she knew, Dr. Basehart was the only person in the lab trailer. The lights were on in his living trailer, but she couldn't see anyone through the windows.

Well, she could find out in the morning. All she wanted to do right now was wash up as best she could and go to bed. She headed for the guest trailer, stretching her arms and bending out the kinks she still felt from her ordeal.

What was that? The sound wasn't much more than a low thud, but the jungle was spooky. Her nerves were raw enough for the sound to make her jump. It came from behind the lab trailer—from a small, windowless shack she'd never noticed before.

There. Another thumping noise. She could feel her skin tingling with fear.

But now she was curious—and suspicious. Dr. Basehart had a strange way of not answering her questions and keeping information to himself. Just what was he not telling? And what might that little shack be hiding?

She stood on her tiptoes and craned her neck to see through the window of Dr. Basehart's lab trailer. He was still in there, busily at work on the samples.

Ducking down so she wouldn't be seen and moving silently, she slipped into the shadows behind the trailer. There she got a clear look at the thrown-together shack that stood in a clear area all by itself. Fresh soil lay on the ground all around it. It could have been an outhouse with a pit dug under it, but it sure seemed big for an outhouse.

Besides, the narrow door was locked shut with not only a padlock but also two hefty slide bolts—all on the outside. Outhouses had little slide bolts on the inside to keep people from bursting in unexpectedly; this one was well secured from the outside to . . . well, to keep someone or something from getting out.

And one other thing: It didn't smell like an outhouse. This shed had a strange, musty smell, like mold or mildew. She wrinkled her nose. Not a good smell.

But it seemed strangely familiar. Where had she smelled it before? She stepped closer, sniffing curiously.

A shriek! Flapping wings, flying feathers! Lila almost jumped out of her skin as a huge macaw fluttered from the roof of the shack, disturbed by her intrusion.

She tried to remain motionless while she found her breath again, her eyes on the rear window of Dr. Basehart's lab trailer. That silly bird must have been making that thumping noise she'd heard, and now it made such a racket she feared she would be discovered.

She could see Dr. Basehart through the window. Apparently he was used to jungle noises. He didn't seem bothered, but just continued cleaning off his work counter. It looked like he might be closing things up for the night. He'd opened a folding partition and was putting some small jars away on a shelf behind it.

Wait a minute. What's that in the room behind the partition? She only caught a glimpse of it before he closed the partition again, but it looked like . . .

CREAK! She flinched, shaking. It was the door to Dr. Basehart's trailer. He was stepping outside. She froze, her mind racing. *What if he sees me back here?*

Click. Dr. Basehart turned out the lights of the lab trailer and closed the trailer door behind him. Maybe he was turning in for the night. Yes, she could hear his footsteps crossing the open space between the three trailers, and then the door to his living trailer squeaked open.

The door slammed shut, and everything went quiet again.

Her heart was still racing—but beginning to slow down. He was gone. She was alone now, hiding in the close, shadowy confines behind his lab.

And she was thinking—not that she *wanted* to think it; it just occurred to her—that if she wanted to, she could take a look inside that trailer. She might be able to figure out what he was working on.

She could also take a peek behind that partition. If nothing else, she could have a look at the bug he'd found in her nose, *if* there really was one. She even remembered that Dr. Basehart kept a flashlight by the door.

Stepping carefully and silently, she peeked around the corner of the lab trailer to be sure he was really gone for the night. She could see one light still on in his living trailer, but then it winked out. Armond Basehart had to be calling it a night.

The thought of taking a look inside the lab trailer became more than a thought; it became a plan.

She built up her courage, drew a deep breath, and then moved like a cat around the lab trailer to its door. It creaked a bit when she opened it, but she got inside without drawing anyone's attention.

Dr. Basehart's emergency flashlight was on a little holder next to the door. She clicked it on, keeping the beam low so it wouldn't be seen, and went to the counter where Dr. Basehart had been working so intently.

The samples were still there, all very orderly: slime from the pit; some other slime she had not seen before; the smear from her nose, still under the microscope; her blood, now distributed into several small vials for testing; and . . .

What is this? She hadn't noticed the glass jar before. Sealed with a lid, it contained a piece of cloth. Somehow it looked familiar. She gave the jar a few turns so she could view it from every side—gray cloth, with a green, chalky dust on it.

Then she remembered. The rag from the Corys'

video! She recalled the images of John Cory using this rag to wipe the golden artifacts from Kachi-Tochetin's tomb. Why would Dr. Basehart want to keep it in a jar?

Oh, wait a minute. She remembered the very first carvy she and her father and brother had seen; it had been hiding in the Corys' tent under a rag just like this one. Maybe that was the connection; Dr. Basehart seemed to want a sample of anything a carvy might touch.

The microscope had its own lamp to illuminate the slide. She found the little switch and clicked it on. Then she peered through the eyepiece and slowly turned the focus wheel.

What in the world? This was no bug. Maybe it was dust, like Dr. Basehart had said. But it was the weirdest looking dust she'd ever seen: thousands of little fuzzy balls—they looked like cockle burrs, or chestnut husks, or sea urchins—with sharp quills sticking out all over them. They looked absolutely wicked.

These were in her *nose*? She shuddered at the thought and clicked off the microscope. She had to know more.

With the flashlight beam low, she moved silently to the partition that divided the trailer in half. Maybe there was nothing important back there after all, but just the fact that Dr. Basehart kept it closed all the time was reason enough for her to want to open it.

She placed her hand on the small plastic handle and slowly drew the partition to the side.

Something glimmered in the beam of her flashlight.

She gasped, her hand over her mouth, frozen in terror and disbelief as a horrible revelation streamed into her mind.

What to do? Where to go?

She had to get out of there. She had to find her father and brother.

She clicked off the flashlight, slipped it back into its little holder, and stole out the trailer door. *Dad, Jay, where are you?*

Dr. Basehart's trailer was still dark. There was no visible activity. She hurried toward her trailer, constantly looking over her shoulder. If she could just get back there and try to act normal—

BUMP! She leaped with a start. The gasp she drew in could have inflated a blimp. She tried not to scream but a small squeak escaped her throat. She'd bumped into someone or some . . . *thing*. It hollered, just as startled as she was, and started stumbling in the dark, trying to recover.

"Shhh!!!" she shushed it.

The wide and startled eyes of her brother gawked back at her. "Lila! What are you doing here?"

She waved her hands to shush him and hissed, "Will you be quiet? You'll wake everybody up!"

"You're all right?" he whispered back, touching her to be sure she was real. "You're still green."

"I'm okay," she answered. Then she started tugging him toward Dr. Basehart's lab. "Come on! I've got to show you something!"

"But Dad's in trouble! The Kachakas have him!"

"We're *all* in trouble!"

They stole quickly into the lab trailer. Lila got the flashlight and then drew back the partition.

Jay took one look into the room beyond and then moaned. "You're right. We're all in trouble."

On two wide shelves against the rear wall were the golden vase, cups, jewelry, figurines—everything—from the Corys' video.

"What are we going to do?" Lila wondered.

CLICK! The sound of the light switch and the sudden flood of light made them gasp and jump and spin around.

There in the doorway, with one hand on the light switch and a gun in the other, was Dr. Armond Basehart. "I thought I heard some noise over here. Looks like I've found two little mice sticking their noses where they don't belong." He got a cunning gleam in his eye. "You've asked a very astute question, Miss Cooper. Now that you know our little secret, just what *are* we going to do?"

EIGHT

Dr. Basehart stepped into the trailer and then beckoned to someone outside. Immediately, Tomás climbed through the door, eyeing the kids grimly, ready to do his boss's bidding.

"So I guess you've figured it out by now," Dr. Basehart said resignedly. "There never was a raid on the Corys' camp. I may as well tell you, the Kachakas can give quite a show of strength and they are excellent hunters, but when it comes to violent raids and murder . . ." He just shook his head.

"So what really happened to the Corys?" Lila asked.

"The same thing that happened to you. The 'Curse of Toco-Rey.' They went crazy, tore up their own camp, and then ran into the jungle like animals. As your brother can tell you, one of them is dead, his bones picked clean by the carvies."

"But what about those graves?" Jay asked.

"Fake, just like the poison darts you found." Dr. Basehart chuckled. "Well, *one* grave is genuine, as was the blood you found in the tent. Another worker of mine, Chico Valles, was killed by a crazed Cory.

We buried him, then created two mock graves so we could tell our little story about a Kachaka attack."

"But why?" Lila wondered.

Dr. Basehart's eyes narrowed. "To settle the whole matter before anyone like you came along and started to ask questions. You and your family were brought here to find the treasure room of Kachi-Tochetin. What happened to the Corys was to be none of your concern."

"But . . ." Lila couldn't fathom Dr. Basehart's callousness. "But these are people, human beings, in trouble! We can't just let them die!"

Dr. Basehart brushed her off. "A few human lives are a small price to pay for what we've discovered."

She became indignant. "No! Listen. If you've found a cure for the curse, then you've got to use it to save them!"

"They are beyond saving, my dear."

"*I* got better!" Then she added, "And I think you know how!"

He weighed that for a moment. "I might. One more experiment would resolve a few problems, though." He shot a glance at Tomás. "Bring the explosives. We'll do this quickly."

Dr. Cooper knew he could not hurry through the swamp if he wanted to get through it at all. So despite the agony of not knowing the fate of his children for a few additional moments, he carefully retraced the Corys' trail markers and picked his way through. Once on solid ground again, he barreled down the trail through the entangling jungle, his arms protecting his face. His legs grabbed distance in long, powerful strides.

When he reached the Corys' devastated campsite he raced right past it, barely giving it a glance. He had to get to the compound. He had to find his kids.

Hidden behind the Corys' sagging tent, Armond Basehart held Jay while Tomás held Lila, their hands over the kids' mouths so they could not cry out. Once he was sure Dr. Cooper was far past, Dr. Basehart prodded the kids with his gun—"Okay, let's go"—and they headed up the same trail their father had come down.

Dr. Cooper pulled his gun as he reached the compound, his eyes alert for trouble. Dawn was approaching. The compound was quiet. There was a light on in Basehart's lab trailer.

Taking cautious, silent steps and pointing his gun skyward, he approached the door of the trailer. Through a window he could see a man bent over the work counter, tinkering with samples and looking through the microscope. Dr. Cooper put his hand on the door handle, then jerked the door open suddenly, aiming his gun inside. "Don't move!"

The man complied and became very still.

"Put your hands on the counter where I can see them."

The man placed both of his hands on the counter, then said pleasantly, "Dr. Cooper. I've been expecting you."

Dr. Cooper stepped through the door, still aiming the gun. "I've been expecting you too, Mr. Stern."

"May I turn around and face you?"

"Hands in the air, please."

The man raised his hands and turned around. It was Mr. Stern from the museum, all right, dressed in jungle fatigues instead of a fancy suit but still the dapper, gray-haired gentleman. "So it seems you've figured out our little ruse."

"I've learned that the Kachakas know nothing of any raid on the Cory camp. They think the Corys are ghosts from the tomb. They've never even seen the treasure and the poison darts they use are quite different from the fake ones your people planted at the Corys' camp—better, actually."

Mr. Stern was impressed. "Very observant. But here's something else for you to note." He nodded toward the clothing Lila had left on the couch. "As you can see, we have your children, so I have plenty of advantage. That gun won't do you much good. You're a reasonable man. Perhaps you'd like to have a discussion instead of a shoot-out?"

Dr. Cooper kept the gun in his hand. "Fine. Let's discuss my children."

Mr. Stern liked that response. "Certainly. Armond Basehart has them. You'll be glad to know that they are both alive and well, and Lila *is* recovering from her illness. Tomás and Juan found her in the ruins and brought her here where Basehart had a chance to run some tests. Thanks to your daughter, we've made some exciting discoveries."

Dr. Cooper tightened his grip on the gun he was aiming at Mr. Stern. "Where are they?"

Mr. Stern smiled, amused. "Now doctor, you know I can't give up my advantage. We haven't had our discussion yet." He looked at his raised hands. "And may I put down my hands?"

Jacob Cooper considered, then replied, "Cross your arms in front of you—and start explaining what you're really up to."

Mr. Stern crossed his arms and relaxed against the counter. "All right. First of all, my name isn't Stern, and second, I don't work for the Langley Art Museum. I have a few friends there who helped me set up our meeting in the museum's work room, but that was purely for the sake of appearances. My real name is—" He stopped himself and smiled. "Well, let me just tell you the name I use in my profession. In all your visits to the Middle East, you've no doubt heard the name Manasseh."

Dr. Cooper had heard the name. "The international weapons dealer?"

The man known as Manasseh nodded. "A supplier of weapons of all kinds to terrorists, revolutionaries, or anyone who wants to start a war. If you have the right kind of money, I don't care whose side you're on."

Dr. Cooper knew he was facing a man with no trace of conscience. "So what do you want with me and my children?"

"Oh, exactly what I hired you for: to pick up

where the Corys left off and find the treasure room of Kachi-Tochetin."

Dr. Cooper was puzzled. "What would a weapons dealer want with ancient artifacts?"

Manasseh laughed. "Not the artifacts, doctor! The *curse* guarding them!"

"*What?*"

Manasseh's eyes sparkled with devious delight. "Imagine entire armies stricken with madness—turning into raving animals, turning and attacking each other instead of the enemy, generals going out of their minds! Whoever possessed such a wonderful biological weapon could win a war without firing a shot!"

Dr. Cooper quickly scanned the work counter behind Manasseh. "So that's what Armond Basehart was working on all this time?"

"Exactly. He acquired the journals of José de Carlon and developed the theory that the curse of Toco-Rey might be due to a rare toxin the Oltecas planted in the tomb. He came to me with his idea. I bought into it, and, well, here we are."

"And you hired Ben Cory and his crew to find the tomb for you."

"And to unwittingly serve as guinea pigs. They entered the tomb, encountered the toxin, and later went berserk, proving our theory. You can imagine our elation! We had discovered a toxin that had remained dormant for a thousand years but still came to life upon contact with human beings. It is the ideal weapon! It can be stored for years—sealed in shell casings, kept in jars, whatever—and still work when we want it to. But our archaeological team was reduced to raging animals, and we still didn't know exactly where the tomb was. Besides, neither Basehart nor I had any intention of going into the tomb ourselves. So . . ."

"You hired me."

Manasseh nodded. "And staged the raid on the Cory camp so you wouldn't know our real intentions."

Dr. Cooper was appalled. "You're a mad man."

That only amused Manasseh further. "No, just a businessman. Thanks to the Corys, we were able to discover a perfect weapon that could devastate an army, a city, or a nation." He pointed to a jar on the counter containing a preserved dead carvy. "And thanks to your daughter, who was affected by the toxin and then recovered, we were able to discover the cure. So we now have a product we can sell to the right people for millions. In a way, there's treasure in the burial tomb of Kachi-Tochetin worth far more than the gold."

Dr. Cooper wasn't entirely impressed. "So what do you intend to do, start a carvy farm?"

Manasseh burst out laughing as if he'd heard a terrific joke. "That's good, doctor! Very good! But let's get to the real discussion here. You want your children, I want your cooperation. Let's cut a deal."

Jacob Cooper said nothing. He just listened.

Manasseh made his pitch. "We need your expertise in further explorations of the tomb and any other sites that might contain the toxin. We'll harvest the toxin, and any treasure you find, you can keep for yourself. You'll be a millionaire, doctor, overnight— *if* you join us, and *if* you keep our little secret."

"Assist you in profiting from the deaths of millions of people? You're talking to the wrong man."

Manasseh only smiled wickedly. "I've heard about your deep moral convictions, Doctor. But I'm willing to wager that your Christian morality can only govern you up to a point. Beyond that, well, as they say, every man has his price."

"I got my Christian morality from God, and He's a far greater treasure than you could ever offer me. I'm afraid I'll have to decline." Dr. Cooper raised the gun threateningly. "Now where are my kids?"

Manasseh eyed him a moment, then tested him. "We can throw in an immediate bonus, a little incentive: How about two million dollars—today?"

Dr. Cooper pulled the hammer back. "Where are they?"

"Two *more* million once you've found the tomb and make it accessible."

Dr. Cooper spoke slowly and clearly. "I strongly suggest you take me to my children."

Lila and Jay stared into the pit near the burial tomb of Kachi-Tochetin, closely guarded by Armond Basehart and Tomás. The morning sunlight was piercing through the trees and the carvies had returned from their night foraging. There were so many of them that their restful muttering and shuffling echoed out of the pit like the hum of a beehive.

"You gotta be kidding!" said Jay.

"Make no sudden moves or noises, and green carvies can be quite indifferent to your presence," said Basehart. "Tomás, the ladder."

Tomás seemed very nervous but obeyed, opening a bundle and removing a long rope ladder.

"Hook it over the wall and lower it down very slowly. Let's not upset our little friends down there."

Tomás anchored the top end of the ladder to the wall, then let the ladder out one rung at a time, lowering it into the pit. The hum of the carvies stayed steady. So far, so good.

"Why do we have to go down there?" Lila asked.

"Oh, indulge me," said Dr. Basehart. "One final little experiment. Tomás here insists that green carvies are harmless. We're going to find out if he's right."

Manasseh seemed to weaken. He'd tried several tempting offers to buy Jacob Cooper's loyalty, but the Christian was unshakable.

"You certainly are a man of conviction."

"Some things are more important than money," Dr. Cooper said simply. "Now we can spend the rest of the day in a deadlock or we can bring everything to a conclusion. It's up to you."

Manasseh thought it over, then nodded. "All right."

"Where is Dr. Basehart?"

"Actually, he and Tomás went into the ruins at first light to gather some more samples. *I* have your children. They're locked up in a shed in back."

Dr. Cooper gestured toward the door with his gun. "Let's go."

Manasseh made his way out under Dr. Cooper's watchful eye. Then he led him around to the back of the trailer where the shed stood, still locked up with a padlock and two slide bolts. "This was rather hurriedly built, I'm afraid. We weren't expecting to house prisoners."

"Open it up."

Manasseh took a key from his pocket and unlocked the padlock. The two bolts slid easily aside, but the door wouldn't budge when he tugged on the handle. He turned to Dr. Cooper, looking apologetic. "As I said, we put this together rather in a hurry."

Dr. Cooper stepped closer and grabbed the door handle. With both of them tugging, the door finally jerked open. It was dark inside. He could tell immediately his kids were not—

OOF! Something hit him from behind with tremendous force, hurling him through the door. The shed had no floor and he fell, tumbling head over heels through empty space until he landed with a soft thud. The dust rose up in a cloud around him, choking him, blinding him. He could feel it grating between his teeth, burning in his nose.

Struggling to his feet in the dim light, he blinked his eyes clear and discovered he'd fallen into a pit about eight feet deep. He could hear the voices of Juan and Carlos above, laughing and chattering. "Very good job," Manasseh told them. "Muy, muy bueno!"

The door slammed shut and the pit went dark except for thin ribbons of light that came through cracks between the boards.

Manasseh had a quick conversation with Juan and Carlos, and then Dr. Cooper could hear the two men walking away. "Sorry to slam the door on you, Dr. Cooper," Manasseh called from outside. "But we can't let any of that fine green dust escape. The stuff is lethal."

Jacob Cooper looked around as his eyes adapted to the dim light. The shed was sealed up with clear plastic and the air inside was murky with green dust. It covered the walls of the pit and lay several inches thick on the pit floor. He was covered with it. He could taste it.

And he wasn't alone. A dead man sat in a corner of the pit, his eyes gone, his jaw hanging open, barely recognizable under a thick layer of green mold that covered his entire body.

"Dr. Cooper," Manasseh called, "may I introduce you to John Cory, the only one of the Cory party we were able to recover and contain. We were lucky enough to find him in the jungle just after he died but before the carvies had a chance to pick his bones clean. And now that Juan and Carlos are gone and we can talk privately, may I also introduce you to the deadly curse of Toco-Rey, that lovely green dust."

Jacob Cooper looked at himself. He looked as if he'd fallen into green chalk.

"I had to laugh at your question about starting a carvy farm," said the ruthless weapons dealer.

"Carvies aren't worth the trouble. Their poison doesn't drive you crazy, it just kills you. But *this* stuff . . . ! Remember the video of the Corys admiring the artifacts they'd brought back? Remember how John Cory wiped them down with a rag, wiping off all the green dust? It's more than dust, Dr. Cooper. It happens to be a spore that can sit dormant for centuries until it infests the respiratory system of a human being. Once you inhale it, it germinates, giving off a toxin that turns you into a raving animal until . . . well, you saw what finally became of Brad Frederick and now John Cory: The spores grow into a deadly fungus that eats you alive. Kachi-Tochetin must have covered his treasure with the stuff, forever guarding it from outsiders. He was a clever old brute, wouldn't you say?"

"Manasseh . . ." Dr. Cooper could hardly talk because of the spores in his throat. "What have you done with my children?"

"You're still worried about *them?* What about yourself?"

"Manasseh!"

He laughed. "Basehart is taking them to the tomb to seal them inside. As you can see, this pit isn't big enough for all of you. The 'deadly curse' of Toco-Rey is too important a secret for kids to know about. They must not leave the jungle to tell the world."

Horror and anger coursed through Dr. Cooper's veins. "NO! Manasseh, go ahead, take me, do what you want, but let them go!"

Manasseh scolded him. "Dr. Cooper, I'm already doing what I want with you. You see, we were hoping we could salvage some spores from the artifacts the Corys brought out, but unfortunately, the carvies found them and licked them clean. Then we thought maybe we could harvest spores from Brad Frederick's body, but the carvies ate all of those too. So, since you won't help us access the tomb to gather more spores, I guess you'll just have to serve as a human incubator right here in this shed! As you can see, John Cory has provided us with a healthy crop of fungus already, and it won't take long before you do the same.

Dr. Cooper could observe John Cory's body being processed from flesh to fungus before his very eyes. "*How* long?"

"Oh, the speed of the infection depends on how much of the spores a person ingests. The Corys wore dust masks in the tomb, but received a light exposure from handling the dusty artifacts back at their camp. Their infection took awhile. Your daughter Lila got only a small dose, so her infection took some time as well. But Dr. Cooper . . ." Manasseh made a *tsk-tsk* sound. "With the heavy dose of spores you've inhaled, I would say you'll be a raving maniac within an hour. As for the kids . . . well, it may be a few more centuries before anyone ever finds out what happened to them." He laughed again, amused by his own cleverness. "Too bad for you it's morning."

"What? What was that?"

"Never mind. You should have taken the deal I

offered you, doctor. You could have looked forward to being alive and rich. Good-bye."

Jay and Lila stood very still on the soft, gooey floor of the pit, afraid to make any sudden moves. All around them, the walls were alive with an unbroken, living layer of green carvies. They were humming and twitching, slithering and sliming over each other's bodies and occasionally flitting from wall to wall.

Tomás stood beside them with a gun in his hand, trying to act like a tough guy but obviously as scared as they were. Dr. Armond Basehart, suddenly cured of his claustrophobia, was just coming to the bottom of the ladder.

"Ah, yes . . ." said Dr. Basehart, shining his flashlight around the walls of the pit. "They just thrive down here, don't they?" He shined his light sideways and found the tunnel. "And that would be the route into the tomb, correct?"

"Yes, sir," said Jay, also pointing his flashlight that direction. "But this time it's full of carvies."

"No matter. A little green slime won't hurt you."

Lila couldn't figure that. "But I thought . . ."

"Trust me. I've learned a lot from your blood tests, young lady—and from your nose. Go ahead." He handed Jay an extra flashlight and then prodded them with the barrel of his gun. They started stepping slowly over the bones and through the carvies toward the tunnel. "Tomás."

Tomás answered, "Sí, señor," but he didn't take a

step or take his eyes off the thousands of little black eyes that looked back at him.

Dr. Basehart opened a bag he carried over his shoulder and brought out a hand-sized explosive charge with an electronic detonator. He put it in Tomás's hand and whispered, "It's preset for five minutes after you activate it. Get them inside, and then . . ." Tomás hesitated. Armond Basehart gave him a nudge. "Go on!"

Tomás pocketed the explosive, clicked on his flashlight, and followed the kids down the tunnel.

Jay and Lila kept moving, crouching down to stay clear of the carvies that clung to the stalactites above, and stepping gingerly on the slime-slickened tunnel floor.

They could see a light shining on the floor ahead of them. It was Lila's flashlight, still lying where she had dropped it. When they reached it, Jay picked it up and handed it to her. "You feeling okay, sis?"

"I'm not sick or crazy, if that's what you mean," she answered. "But we're not doing okay, not at all."

Jay looked back at Tomás. "Why are we down here?"

Tomás waved the gun at him. "Just keep moving." Then Tomás looked back.

Dr. Basehart stood in the pit, still watching them go. "Farther, Tomás."

Unhappily, Tomás waved his gun at the Cooper children. "Farther. Into the tomb."

"Why do you listen to him, anyway?" Jay asked.

Tomás smiled weakly. "Mucho dinero, muchacho. Much money."

They came to the hallway that circled the inner chamber of the pyramid. This was as far as Jay and Dr. Cooper had gotten last time. Jay examined the intricate carvings in the wall—the ones they had guessed might be a warning not to proceed farther.

"How you doing, sis?" Jay asked again.

"I'm all right, don't worry," she insisted.

"Go on, get back farther," said Tomás.

The kids walked down the narrow stone hallway, still stepping around and crouching under resting carvies.

"I think Dad was right," said Jay, exploring the passage with the beam of his flashlight. "This hallway must go clear around the pyramid with an inner chamber in the middle."

"So maybe there's a door somewhere to get inside."

Tomás watched the kids recede down the hallway, then called back up the tunnel, "They are inside!"

Dr. Basehart, waiting at the bottom of the pit, answered back, "Very good, Tomás. You may proceed."

Tomás started fumbling with his gun, his flashlight, and whatever he had in his pocket while trying to keep an eye on the kids.

Dr. Basehart quickly reached into his bag, brought out another explosive charge, and looked around for a bare surface of stone on which to place it.

Suddenly, he heard a whisper from above. "Basehart! Basehart, can you hear me?"

Armond Basehart scurried to the center of the pit

and looked up. It was Manasseh! "Have you taken care of Cooper?"

Manasseh made an "okay" sign with his fingers. "Tucked neatly away in the shed. Where are the children?"

Basehart smiled wickedly. "Inside the pyramid." He held up his explosive charge and grinned. "It's going perfectly."

Manasseh smiled, very pleased. "Then let's be rid of them."

Basehart hurried to the tunnel entrance, anchored the charge, and set the detonator. "Tomás, you are far too trusting," he whispered to himself.

On the ground above, Manasseh held a small radio transmitter in his hand. "I hate to share, Dr. Basehart."

He pressed a button.

Dr. Basehart suddenly saw a red light on the detonator.

The ground shook with a mighty explosion. Smoke, dust, pulverized rock and liquefied carvies shot out of the pit like a geyser.

The sound of the explosion rang through the stone hallway like a bell. Tomás was knocked off his feet and across the stony floor, his own unarmed explosive still in his hand. Jay and Lila dropped to the floor with their arms over their heads as the earth shook beneath their feet.

Standing in the jungle above, the man called Manasseh watched the dust and debris settle and smiled pleasantly, satisfied that the secret of the world's most hideous biological weapon was now safe with him alone. He slipped the little transmitter into his pocket and started hiking back through the ruins.

Dr. Cooper had tested the walls of the pit for handholds, any way to climb out. He'd tried jumping a few times in an effort to grab the ledge above, but the soft ground broke away in his hand and he fell back, kicking up more of the green dust.

Next to him, the body of John Cory had all but disappeared under the rapidly growing fungus. Every time Dr. Cooper moved, more green fungus puffed around him.

His nose and throat burned. He could imagine the spores burrowing into his nasal membranes and throat lining. He was getting dizzy. Disoriented. Scared.

Jay and Lila ran back to help Tomás to his feet, and then they all raced up the tunnel, stepping around dead and stunned carvies, shining their light beams through the dust and smoke. When they reached the end of the tunnel, their worst fear was confirmed: the tunnel was blasted shut.

They were trapped.

NINE

The kids. The tomb. The curse.

The cure.

Come on, Cooper. Think! Think! You've got to find a way out of here. You've got to save your kids.

He felt like the ground was moving beneath his feet. He planted his hand against the dusty, dirty wall of the pit to steady himself.

A raving maniac within an hour? He could feel his mind start to spin even now. Millions of little spores were busy.

The cure. There was a cure. Manasseh said so. But what?

"Too bad for you it's morning," he had said, but what did he mean?

"Thanks to your daughter . . . we were able to discover the cure."

Dr. Cooper's mind wandered. He began to stare at the green, chalky walls and the rapidly vanishing remains of John Cory. Fear began to course through him. *I'm finished. I'm going to die!*

NO! He shook his head and forced himself to think.

Too bad for you it's morning. A carvy in a jar. Carvy poison doesn't make you crazy, it only kills you.

Too bad for you it's morning. What happens in the morning? What *can't* happen in the morning?

Wait. Wait. Morning slugs. The slugs are green in the morning, green and docile. They've been eating all night.

Green?

What did Manasseh say about the artifacts?

The carvies licked them clean.

And what did he say about Brad Frederick's dead body? The carvies had eaten all the spores on it.

They'd found a carvy underneath a rag in the Cory tent. The Corys had used those rags to wipe the green dust off the artifacts. The carvy could have been attracted by the dust on the rags.

Jacob Cooper prayed, *Dear Lord, keep my mind steady. Help me to think!*

Yes! It had to be: The spores must be like candy to the carvies.

So what does that mean?

Why don't the spores kill the carvies?

The carvies must be immune to them. They get happy and docile and turn green, but they don't go crazy and die.

Lila helped Dr. Basehart and Manasseh find the cure.

Too bad for you it's morning.

The yellow slugs must carry the *antitoxin*. But how did Lila get a dose of it?

He had a hunch. There were pieces missing. But it could be the answer. It had to be the answer, there was so little time.

Dr. Cooper's breath was coming in deep chugs through his clenched teeth. His fingers were curled like claws.

No, this pit isn't going to hold me! I'm going to get out of here! WITH GOD'S HELP I'M GOING TO—

Without thinking, with a loud cry and a huge, semicrazed leap, he shot out of the pit and clamped two iron-strong hands onto the frame around the shed door. With a growl, several kicks, and a violent wrenching, he tore the door loose, snapping off the slide bolts and sending the padlock spinning into the weeds. He was free. He moved out in front of the trailers, groping about in the dark, trying to think, trying to plan.

Uh-oh. He could see Juan and Carlos bursting out of their little hut with rifles in their hands. They must have heard all the racket.

No problem. They took one look at him, screamed, and ran, first in frightened circles, and then to their land rover.

"Hey!" he called.

They didn't even look back, but cranked up the old machine and roared down the rutted road toward civilization.

He didn't know what had scared them, and he didn't have time to think about it. Only one thought kept pounding in his hazy mind. Get to the Kachaka village!

With the speed of a gazelle, he bounded up the trail toward the ruins.

The man who called himself Manasseh walked along the Avenue of the Dead briskly, humming a happy little tune and thinking up his next move. He figured he could hire Juan and Carlos to harvest the spores from the shed—after the two incubators were fully used up, of course. He would have to devise airtight containers in which to store the spores as well as a way to measure them out and weigh them for marketing.

Then he would have to figure out a neat and clean way to dispose of Juan and Carlos. Perhaps they, too, should become incubators. As always, the secret had to be protected.

He stopped. He thought he saw movement in the bushes near an immense stone head, a likeness of a past king, no doubt. He drew his pistol from a holster at his side. He didn't like having an animal sneaking around that close, especially when he didn't know what kind of animal it was.

But nothing moved. He relaxed, put away the pistol, and quickened his step. He did not like this place. Too many things could go wrong, there were too many unknowns.

A scream! A pouncing figure struck him from behind before he had time to react. He was on the flat pavement stones, staring up at a green face, flaming eyes, bared teeth.

His screams echoed across the dead ruins for a quick, terrible moment, and then fell silent.

"We are going to die!" Tomás wailed, no longer the tough guy. He'd stuffed the explosive charge back in his coat pocket without thinking.

"Hey, come on," said Jay. "Get a grip! We haven't even weighed our options!"

They were huddled in the dark hallway under the pyramid, acutely aware that a man-made mountain of limestone lay between them and freedom.

"The tunnel we came through can't be the only way out of here," Jay insisted. "The priests got in another way. Dad and I were theorizing about that."

Lila was already exploring down the hallway. "Let's have a look."

They headed down the hallway, and Tomás followed timidly behind. As their lights swept over the cold stone walls, the sounds of their footsteps and breathing resonated up and down the long, narrow passage. The hallway, only six feet wide and just high enough to walk in, was laid out in a big square, tracing the shape of the pyramid but providing no way to reach whatever rooms might be inside. They explored it carefully as they worked their way around, finding a few primitive stone tools, some items of jewelry but no other passageways.

Then, when they rounded the third corner, they found a massive pile of rocks that appeared to have fallen in from above.

"What is this?" Tomás asked. "A cave-in?"

Lila studied the wall. "Look here, Jay. Slots in the wall, just like a ladder."

Jay used his light to follow the ladder slots up to the ceiling. "Yeah, and look where they go: That used to be a way out."

Lila's heart sank. "But it's full of rocks."

Jay was not happy about his conclusion. "After they buried the king, they must have filled in the entrance to this level of the pyramid."

"We will run out of air!" Tomás whined. "We will starve to death!"

Jay and Lila paid him no attention but conferred again.

"The Corys found the treasure room," Jay mused.

"And we haven't," Lila added. "Which means they got in and out of here a totally different way. Remember what Dad said? He thought the tunnel we used was dug out by the Oltecas. The Corys thought the tunnel they found was dug out by José de Carlon. There *has* to be another tunnel somewhere!"

"And it has to lead into the treasure room."

"So if we find the treasure room we're bound to find a way out through the other tunnel."

Jay pointed his flashlight at the wall. "Is there any soft mortar along that wall? Tomás, help us look!"

They backtracked through the hallway, searching the inside wall with their lights.

"We're looking for old mortar, for cracks. . . ."

Jay instructed their captor-turned-helper. "Somewhere there has to be an entrance to the tomb that was sealed up after the king was buried. After a thousand years the mortar should be soft."

They moved along quickly, tapping and poking at the wall as they went. *Tick, tick, tap.* The wall produced a solid, stony sound as they struck it. They kept moving, kept tapping.

THUNK. About halfway down the hall, Lila's flashlight hit something soft, and she made a slight dent in the decaying, powdery surface. "Hey."

"This could be it," said Jay. He picked up one of the old tools they'd found and used it to chip at the soft spot in the wall. The material broke away freely, falling to the floor in dusty, jagged chunks.

"Hurry," said Tomás. "Please hurry!"

Lila got into it, chipping and gouging with a sharp rock. Tomás found another rock and started bashing away, driven by fear.

The leaves and branches of the jungle raced by his face in a blur; the whole world kept tilting, first one way, then the other. Dr. Cooper felt he was running on the deck of a ship in a storm.

Dear Lord, keep me steady. Help me get to the Kachaka village.

The Pyramid of the Sun was right in front of him, so he must have passed through the gates of Toco-Rey, though he had no memory of it. The mind of an animal kept forcing its way into his head. He felt like a panther, running with the wind, hungry for blood, superpowered by a rage that made everything around him an enemy to be destroyed. His breath came in deep, guttural chugs. He had to force himself to think, to remember who he was and what he was doing. Though he felt amazingly strong, part of him knew he was getting very, very sick.

He had a hunch. Sometimes he forgot what it was, but he kept running for the Kachaka village anyway, trusting God would bring the memory back.

"You are Dr. Jacob Cooper," he kept telling himself. "Run to the village. Run to the village."

He raced up the Avenue of the Dead. In his desperate struggle to hold on to his mind he didn't notice the blood or the remains of what had been the world's most ruthless weapons dealer. He ran right by without slowing down.

Jay struck another blow against the wall, and this time the mortar and stones crumbled, falling into a cavity on the other side. "All right! We're through!" He poked his flashlight into the hole and peered through. "Yeah. There's a chamber in there."

"Can you see anything?" Lila asked.

Jay swept his light back and forth, probing the darkness. "Whoa . . . oh wow . . ."

"What is it?" Tomás demanded.

Jay turned to them, jubilant. "It's the treasure room! We've found it!"

They bashed and chipped and pounded with even greater determination, enlarging the hole, pushing the old stones and gray mortar into the chamber beyond. As soon as the hole was big enough to squeeze through, Jay did just that, crouching down, going one leg first, then his body, then the other leg.

He found himself in a large, square chamber with carved pillars at each corner. The ceiling was at least fifteen feet above him. A huge, stone coffin took up the center. "Okay. Come on in."

Lila hopped through the hole. Tomás poked his head in first, made doubly sure it was safe, and then squeezed through the hole with a little more difficulty.

All three were astounded. The walls around them held intricately carved figures of warriors, kings, and fierce, toothy gods. The four pillars had huge faces, all looking inward toward the coffin; they probably represented Kachi-Tochetin and his family.

The coffin in the center of the room was a huge box of limestone on a stone pedestal. It, too, was intricately carved with faces, suns, moons, gods, and plants that swirled in a continuous pattern all around its four sides. Carved into the lid was the stern face of Kachi Tochetin, superimposed over the sun so that the sun's rays seemed to emanate from the king himself.

But the real eye-catcher was the *treasure*. All around the room, stacked up high against the walls and taking up much of the floor, was the wealth of Kachi-Tochetin. Masks of gold and turquoise, necklaces and breastplates, piles and piles of coins and beads, golden cups, plates, vases, idols.

On a ledge around the room were more small golden images of Oltecan gods the Corys had referred to, positioned to stand guard over the treasure and the remains of the king.

Then came a gruesome discovery: In each corner, at the base of each carved pillar, was a length of chain. And on the floor, in a dismal, helter-skelter pile, were bones. Tomás let out a gasp of fear. Jay and Lila went to take a closer look.

"The guards the Corys talked about," said Jay. "They must have been chained to the pillars to guard the king."

"Buried alive!" said Lila.

Now Jay understood. "These must be the mukai-tochetin that the Kachaka chief talked about. They really were buried with the king!"

Tomás picked up a golden vase. He immediately put it down in disgust when he saw the green dust it left on his hands. "Eughh!" He slapped his hands against his pantlegs, stirring up a green cloud.

Now the kids noticed too. It was very dusty in here. A thick layer of green dust was all over everything. They'd left footprints in it. Everything they touched left a handprint—and left green dust on their hands.

"Wow," said Jay, slapping the top of the king's coffin and raising another cloud of dust. "Weird stuff."

"The Corys talked about this dust too," Lila remembered. "They were wiping it off the artifacts in that video—" She stopped. The smell in this place was oddly familiar. She tried to remember where she'd smelled it before. Thoughts came to her; memories. "Jay . . ."

She looked at her brother. He'd scratched his nose and left a green smudge. Just then, Tomás sneezed and wiped his face with his hand. That only drove more dust up his nose and he sneezed again, stomping his foot and raising even more dust.

"Jay!"

He was wiping off an artifact with his shirt sleeve. She could see the tiny particles dancing around in the beam of his flashlight.

"Jay, stop!"

He stopped. "Huh? What's the matter?" Then he made a little face, rolling his eyes and teetering slightly. "Whoa! Did we just have an earthquake?"

The Kachaka village! Jacob Cooper burst out of the jungle and recognized the small huts of grass and sticks, the ramshackle, plank structures, the busy people. . . .

He stumbled and fell in the grass, his head reeling. *WhydidIcomeherewhatfor* . . .

He heard excited shouts and people approaching. *Come on Coop gedup you godda meg sense to these peeble* . . .

With great strength he leaped to his feet again. "Where da chief? Lemme talk gotta get him or here!"

The women and children took one look at him, screamed, and ran away, wailing, waving their arms, sounding an alarm.

Fierce anger coursed through him. *Whatza matter widese peeble? I'll kill them! Kill them all!* He ran after them, hands like claws, teeth bared. "Stop you iddits! Whatzamatta wi'yu?"

He stopped. What in the world was he doing? *Oh man, Lord, I'm losing it! Help me!* He dropped to his knees in the grass, trying to think, trying to clear his head. *Calm down. Control, control! You have to get . . . you have to get . . . what do I have to get?*

Then he heard a familiar, angry voice. "Doctor Jacob Cooper, the stupid American!"

He looked up. It was the chief, whose angry expression turned to one of fear the moment Dr. Cooper raised his head. The chief muttered, gawked at him, started backing away.

Dr. Cooper tried to speak clearly. "Chief Yoaxa . . ."

Yoaxa looked at the others who cowered behind him, staring at the weird animal that had burst into their village. He started hollering an explanation to them. Dr. Cooper couldn't understand it, but he easily heard the word *mukai-tochetin* used over and over again.

Jacob Cooper struggled to his feet. "Please . . ." His voice came out like a growl. "I need . . . I need . . ."

"Go away!" the chief hollered. "You are mukai-tochetin! I knew it all along!"

Some warriors came running with rifles, spears, and blowguns, ready to use them all.

That brought a new fit of rage Jacob Cooper could hardly control. "You fools! Can't I make you understand!" he growled. He was clenching his fists, shaking them at these stupid people—

He stopped, horrified, at the sight of his hands.

They were lizard green.

TEN

Lila's voice trembled with fear. "Jay . . . I think it's the dust!"

He looked at her dully. "Huh?"

She ran over and grabbed his arm. "Listen to me! Remember what Dr. Basehart said? He said he learned a lot from my blood samples—and from my *nose!* You remember that?"

Jay had trouble remembering. "Your nose?"

"Jay, I've smelled this stuff before! I smelled it coming from a shack behind Dr. Basehart's lab, and—are you listening to me?—I smelled it on an orchid near where we found the pit. This dust was on that orchid! I snorted it right up my nose, do you understand?"

He looked at her with impatience. "What are you trying to do, scare me?"

She gripped his arm tighter. "You feel afraid?"

He jerked his arm away. "NO! There's nuddin wrong wid me!"

"Jay! It wasn't the slime from the carvies that made me green and crazy! It was this dust! Dr. Basehart had samples of it in his lab. He had that rag the Corys used to wipe off the artifacts! He had a

128

sample from my nose—Jay, you should have seen it under the microscope! It was like hundreds of little spiky monsters, that's what this dust is!"

He looked directly at her now. She seemed to be getting through. "It's the dust?"

She looked at him carefully, noticing the glazed look in his eyes and the way he tottered as if drugged. "Jay, it's happening to you! The same thing that happened to me is happening to *you!*"

He got defensive. "You look okay."

She tried to keep from crying, but fear still brought tears to her eyes. "I got better somehow, Jay. I don't know how it works. Maybe you only get it once, like the measles."

Jay tried to listen to his sister. Her words were so garbled and there was such a rushing noise in his ears. The floor still seemed to be moving. "Lila . . . Maybe we bedder ged ouda here."

She looked all around. "Jay, we can't. There isn't any way out. I mean, I can't see it, I can't find it."

"We havetuh fine it."

She grabbed his arm to steady him. "Jay—"

He jerked away with a growl. "Leggo! You don't touch me!"

He's losing it, she thought. He's going to do something really crazy if I don't—

"Lila!"

"What?"

Jay stared at a corner of the room. She followed his gaze and saw a pile of bones and the black, rusty chain that had once held the doomed guard.

"You better chain me up," Jay said. "Chain me up before I really go nuts."

129

The thought was unbearable. "Jay . . ."

"Do it!" he growled. "Before I can't think straight anymore!"

He stumbled over to the pillar and flopped against it, his breath raspy, his eyes getting wild. She grabbed the chain and looped it around his body, his arms, his legs.

He began to struggle against her. "What are you doing?"

"It's okay, Jay. Don't worry!"

"Quit it! Let me go!" he growled at her. Then he tried to grab her. She ducked sideways, barely avoiding his flailing arms and clawlike fingers. He was dazed, disoriented. She jumped in close to finish looping and twisting the chain into a knot behind his back.

For just a moment his mind returned. "Get out of here, sis."

She looked all around the room. "I don't see the way out."

"FIND IT!" he screamed at her, his eyes ablaze with animal anger. He tried to lunge at her but the chain held him fast. He fell back against the pillar as the chain rattled against the stone.

Lila hurried around the room, looking everywhere. How? How did the Corys do it? How did they get in and out? She could see their footprints in the dust all over the floor, but there were so many she couldn't tell which direction they'd come from or where they were going. She checked in one corner, then another, then she climbed over some of the treasure to check against a wall.

Nothing.

She ran to the next corner. Maybe there was a movable panel, or a scrape mark on the floor showing where the exit was, or—

TOMÁS! He suddenly leaped to his feet from behind a large chest, a golden vase in his hands. His face and hands were covered with green dust, and his eyes looked absolutely wild! She jumped backward, horrified. She'd forgotten about him in her panic about Jay.

He leaned toward her, teetering a little, his shoulders hunched, his mouth stretched into a toothy sneer. "Come here, señorita. Come here!"

Her eyes shot to the hole in the wall, the only way in or out of this room that she knew of.

Unfortunately, he was standing right next to it.

Dr. Cooper took a step forward and all the Kachakas took a step backward. His mind kept flipping back and forth, and he couldn't stop it: *Kill them.* No, they're people. *Kill them.* No, help them, make them understand. *KILL THEM!*

"NO, DEAR GOD, NO!" he finally cried in anguish. "Help me, Lord! Help me to think—"

The Lord answered his prayer. His mind cleared, if only for a moment. He looked at Chief Yoaxa, who had several armed warriors at his side. "Chief . . . where's your daughter María?"

Instantly, every rifle, blowgun, ax, and spear was aimed at him.

He raised his hands, pleading with them. "Don't!

Don't shoot me!" He just couldn't keep his voice from sounding growly. "I needa ask María a question . . . jus' one question."

The chief thought for less than a moment and wagged his finger at him. "Oh, no. No, you cannot fool me! María is not yours! You cannot have her!"

ANGER. Dr. Cooper gritted his teeth and prayed. He knew he would tear Chief Yoaxa limb from limb if he didn't control himself. He strained to say it clearly. "Just one question."

Now the chief took a rifle himself. "I don't care if you are mukai-tochetin, I shoot you anyway!"

Slowly, one difficult word at a time, Cooper asked, "Did María shoot my daughter Lila with a poison dart?"

That got a reaction. The chief lowered his rifle and looked at his men. It seemed they knew something.

"Chief . . ." Jacob Cooper knew the man was almost impossible to reason with, but he had to try. "Your daughter María had a blowgun when we found her. She shot . . ." His mind fluttered. He struggled to find it again. "She shot at my son and me. If she shot at us, maybe she shot at Lila." The chief and his men looked at each other. They knew something, Dr. Cooper could see it! His next words sounded like the roar of a lion. "TELL ME!"

"Yes!" came the answer, but not from any of the warriors. The voice came from beyond them.

It was the voice of María. She pushed her way forward until her mother and brothers grabbed her and held her back, but she could see Dr. Cooper, and he could see her. "Dr. Cooper, yes, I shot your daughter with a dart. I thought she was going to kill me!"

Jacob Cooper shot a glance at Chief Yoaxa, who looked a bit cornered. "She . . ."

"WHAT?" came the lion's voice again. "TELL ME!"

"She did have a blowgun," Chief Yoaxa continued. "The one you found didn't belong to any of us. We learned it was hers."

With a roar so loud it startled the men and brought terrified screams from the women, Dr. Cooper charged forward, waving his arms for people to get out of his way. They got out of his way, all right. They didn't want to be anywhere near him.

"Wait!" the chief hollered, following after him. "Where are you going?"

Dr. Cooper didn't answer. He just kept running past the huts and shacks until he came to the end of the village. He rounded a corner and there was the cage full of carvies, as yellow and fierce and poisonous as ever.

Lila backed away, her hands out in front of her. "Now . . . now Tomás, listen to me . . ."

He just growled back at her and threw the golden vase aside with a crash and a clang. He was going to come after her, that was easy to see. She backed away some more. Her only hope was to lead him away from that hole.

With an animal roar he leaped over the treasure

133

and came after her, growling with every breath. She ran around the big stone coffin and he chased her, scuffing and slipping in the green dust, sending up clouds of the stuff. She ran for the hole in the wall—at least she'd lured Tomás away from it—and dove through headfirst, tumbling and rolling out the other side into the hallway. She got to her feet and ran. It would take him a moment or two to squeeze through behind her, which would buy her some time . . . to do what?

She ran first. She'd think of something later.

The carvies flitted from side to side in their cage, slapping against the wire mesh, chirping, hissing, arching their backs. They were bright yellow, angry, and throwing slime every time they fluttered their fins. A whole night had passed and they hadn't eaten a thing.

Jacob Cooper had already made up his mind. He was going to die anyway and go stark raving mad before that. He had nothing to lose.

He found a small empty cage about the size of a suitcase. It would work perfectly. He grabbed it, then went to the carvies' cage and started to untwist the crinkly old wire that held it shut.

The chief and his men came running around the corner, but stopped dead in their tracks the moment they saw what he was up to. "He is crazy for sure!" the chief exclaimed.

"They won't hurt him," said Manito. "Will they?"

"They will hurt *us!*" the chief reminded him.

They scurried backward, still watching, spell-bound. They'd never seen this done before.

Dr. Cooper got the wire undone. He opened the little door on the cage he was carrying, then yanked the door of the big cage open, took a breath . . .

And jumped inside.

Slap! Splat! Flop! The carvies descended on him like angry hornets, sliming him, slapping against him, slithering over his back, his arms, his head. Their shrieks sounded like all the rats in the world getting stepped on, their slime burned like fire on his hands, his neck, his face, and he couldn't help but scream and gasp from the pain. One clamped onto his ear like a sticky pancake and started biting him. He thought he would pass out. He reached up, yanked it loose—it felt like a sticky, slimy, flattened water balloon in his hand—and threw it into the small cage. It flopped and fluttered around, trying to get out. Then he grabbed another from his arm and another from his side and both went into the cage. He stayed hunched over, one hand holding the cage, the other arm around his head to protect his eyes. He needed more of these critters, many more.

His world was reeling. All he could see was cage wire and carvies moving in waves past his eyes. The sight made him dizzy. He stretched out the hand holding the cage and three more carvies slapped against his arm like wet pancakes fired from a sling-shot. He peeled them off with his other hand and threw them into the little cage, slamming the door shut.

That should do it. That should be plenty. He got

135

the big cage door open and, with carvies still crawling on his back, shoulders, legs, and head, he took off running.

The Kachaka village looked strangely deserted. Every last person must be hiding.

And with good reason. It was a bizarre sight, this wild green man running through the village with hissing, chirping, yellow slugs stuck all over him. At least a hundred more fluttered above and behind him, chasing him like angry hornets.

Lila ducked around the first corner in the hallway, spotted a piece of stone, and grabbed it to use as a weapon. Then she pressed herself tightly against the wall, clicking off her flashlight. Hiding in the dark, she could hear Tomás squeeze through the hole and flop into the hall. She saw no beam from a flashlight. He must be too crazy to think of using one. His footsteps started coming her way. What to do? What to do?

"Señorita!" he hollered like a drunken man, his voice like gravel. "Señorita, come here! I'm going to get you, muchachita!"

She waited. He got closer, his feet shuffling, dragging along in the dark. His voice sounded like it was inside a huge bell. "I'll get you . . . and I'll . . . I'll . . ."

She didn't care to hear his plans. The instant his stubbly, sweating, disheveled head appeared around the corner, she smacked it hard with the stone. He fell sideways. She slipped around him and ran back toward the treasure room. Maybe there was time to find the way out. Maybe.

The carvies in the cage were shrieking and bashing against the sides, trying to get out. The carvies overhead were swooping down and slapping at him. The carvies on his body were hanging on, looking for some bare skin so they could bite him. Dr. Cooper just kept running with powerful strides through the ruins until he spotted the Pyramid of the Sun in the center of Toco-Rey. From there, a left turn would take him to the burial tomb of Kachi-Tochetin.

He wasn't dead. That thought did occur to him. As a matter of fact, he was feeling better. The slime wasn't burning quite as much, and best of all, his mind was clear. He knew who he was, where he was going, and why. Praise God, his hunch was correct: the poisonous slime of the *caracole volante* and the toxin from the spores canceled each other out. Lila had recovered because María had shot her with a poison dart, just a big enough dose to neutralize the spore toxin.

Which made Dr. Cooper wonder, how much of this slime is enough, and how much is too much? Right now he was getting an abundant dose of slug slime. Would the load of spores he carried in his body be enough to counteract it?

All he could do was hope and keep running.

Lila clambered through the wall into the treasure room and got a terrible scare when Jay—at least it used to be Jay—growled and snapped at her, pulling against the chain with the ferocity of a junkyard dog. If that chain should break loose . . .

She was trapped in this place with two mad animals. There had to be a way out! She climbed over the treasure, searching the walls, looking for cracks, for chinks, for a hidden door, for a hatchway, *anything*. How did the Corys do it? How did they get in here?

A howl echoed up the hallway outside, and then galloping footsteps. Tomás was out there hunting for her. It was only a matter of time before he found her here.

And then it would be too late.

As Dr. Cooper ran toward the burial temple, he was glad to see that the carvies chasing him had finally vented their anger or had gotten tired. They'd given up the chase, and even the ones still clinging to him were losing interest. Two let go of his back and fluttered into the bushes.

Well, he thought. Of course. They were crabby because they were hungry, so let them get something to eat.

He dashed through the jungle, made some quick turns along the trail near the burial temple, and finally reached the pit.

He stopped. His heart sank. The pit was still smoking from the blast that had caved it in. Looking over the wall, he saw nothing but rubble and shreds of dead carvies. Apparently Armond Basehart had succeeded in sealing the tomb.

But Jacob Cooper had been expecting this and was already working on another hunch, another theory. The question was, How did Lila come in contact with the spores in the first place? What did she do? Where did she go that no one else did?

He dashed back the way he'd come. He was pretty sure he knew the answer.

Lila rested her elbows on the stone coffin and clenched her hands together as she prayed, "Oh Lord, what am I missing? How do I get out of here? How do I save Jay? How did I get better?"

Her leg felt cold, as if in a draft. She reached down near the floor with her hand and felt cold air coming from somewhere.

Somewhere under the coffin? She probed around the stone pedestal the coffin was sitting on. Yes! There was definitely cold air coming into the room through a crack between the coffin and the pedestal. A very tight crack. Maybe the pedestal was hollow. Maybe there was a passageway under the coffin!

She put her hands on the coffin's edge and pushed against it sideways. It wiggled only about a sixteenth of an inch. She moaned. The coffin was carved from solid stone! She couldn't push it sideways, and she knew she would never be able to lift it!

The orchids! Where were they?

Dr. Cooper doubled back on the trail and finally found the spot where Lila had left the main trail to smell orchids on their first trip here. He knew it was a desperate guess, but it seemed reasonable: The Corys had orchids in a vase in their camp. Lila had found the same sort of orchids growing in the ruins and gone off the trail to sniff them. If she got spores in her nose from those orchids, it could be because the Corys had already passed by that spot and had unknowingly spread the spores from their clothing, their hands, or the artifacts. If there was another way into the tomb, it could be near those orchids.

There they were, over by that old, crumbling wall! Dr. Cooper made a quick dash through the thick growth. This was the place, all right. Now. Was there any sign of a tunnel, a passageway? He started moving along the wall. He thought he saw the signs of a trail the Corys might have cut.

He was hit from the side! He tumbled through the branches and tangles as the cage of carvies flew from his hand. Growling! Snapping! Not again! Ben Cory, wild as a tiger, green as a gator, teeth bared, went for his throat. Dr. Cooper fought back, twisting, and kicking.

Lila tried to rock the coffin. It didn't move. She tried to lift it and discovered that was out of the question. She tried to push it sideways again, and it wiggled just a little. Maybe that was it: sideways. Maybe it rolled or pivoted or—

She heard a growl and spun to see Tomás squeezing through the hole, his mouth drooling, his skin turning green, his eyes full of menace.

ELEVEN

Ben Cory had pinned Dr. Cooper and was trying to bite him, claw him, choke him. Cory was amazingly strong, but Jacob Cooper was still just as green as his opponent and still supercharged with enough toxin-induced strength to throw the wild man off and roll free.

The tunnel! He was stunned. He was on his belly in the brush in the middle of a fight, but he'd found it, dark, deep, and round like a gopher hole.

Ben Cory came at him again, staggering, growling, drooling!

Time to end this. The cage of carvies was close by. Dr. Cooper lunged through the brush, grabbed it, and leaped to his feet. He turned just as Ben Cory came at him—and he smashed the cage down over Ben Cory's head. Cory's head broke through the mesh and into the cage and the carvies pounced. The wild man screamed, spinning around, pushing and banging against the cage, trying to get free while the venomous slugs clamped onto his head.

Dr. Cooper had no time to waste. He tackled Ben Cory, flipped the cage door open, and plucked a carvy from Cory's head with each hand. "Come on, guys, I need you below!" They didn't want to go and shrieked and fluttered to get away as they hung from his fists by their tails. He held them firmly and they went with him as he scurried down the tunnel.

He had no light with him and just pushed ahead through the dark, his arm out in front to feel his way along. José de Carlon's men did a good job. The walls of the tunnel were smooth and consistent, and there were no hazardous bumps or dips. They could have dug a little more headroom, though. Dr. Cooper had to crouch to get through.

Lila was careful to keep her distance from Jay, who seemed ready to chomp a piece out of her if she got close enough. On the other side of the room, Tomás squeezed through the hole in the wall and tumbled to the floor.

She grabbed a tall gold vase from a stone ledge and cradled it in her hands, ready to hit a homer with Tomás's head if she had to. "Tomás, you come near me and I'll knock your block off!"

"Get her, Tomás!" Jay hollered. "Get her!"

Tomás got to his feet but hesitated when he saw the vase in Lila's hands. Then cunning began to show through those crazed eyes, and he smiled a crooked, wicked smile. "Oh, you godda use a weapon? Know me, I godda weapon too, know that?" He reached into his coat pocket and brought out the explosive charge with the detonator attached. "Dr. Basehart give me—to kill you!"

Oh no. Could a mad man be reasoned with? "Tomás . . . Don't do anything stupid. Give me that bomb."

He laughed a deep growly laugh and pressed a little button on the detonator. A red display flashed on: *5:00, 4:59, 4:58, 4:57* . . . "You get away? No you don't!"

He lunged for Lila. She ran around the coffin, slipping in the dust and almost getting grabbed by her brother who was still trying to work himself loose from the chain. *Don't lose it, Lila! Don't panic!* Tomás came the other way around the coffin to head her off. She scrambled over the top of it, dropping the vase on the floor. Tomás leaped over the coffin to grab her but she ran around to the other side again, squeezing past her brother who nearly reached her. "Lord God . . . if you've got a way out of this, I'd be glad to hear it!"

"Lila!" came a voice from nowhere. "Lila, are you all right?"

She knew that voice. "DADDY!"

"Lila! Where are you?"

Tomás heard the voice, too, and stiffened with anger. "Where? *Where?*"

"Where are you?" Lila called.

Dr. Cooper had no idea. All he knew was he'd come up through the tunnel to a flat stone surface that seemed like it might move, but didn't. With one hand hanging onto the hissing, flapping carvies, he only had one hand with which to explore or push. "I'm under a slab of stone. Can you see where it is?"

Lila looked at the pedestal under the coffin. Her father's voice seemed to be coming from there.

In the moment she looked away, Tomás lunged for her.

He didn't see the vase lying on the floor in front of him. He tripped on it, sailed through the air, and slammed into the coffin at full speed. It pivoted with a stony rumble as he rolled into a stack of gold cups and utensils. The bomb flew from his flailing hand and skittered across the floor; the display still blinked the shrinking time.

The pedestal was hollow. With the coffin spun cockeyed and leaving a gap, Dr. Cooper was able to poke his head into the middle of all-out chaos.

"Daddy, it's a bomb!" Lila screamed, pointing at the device.

He jumped out of the tunnel to run to her.

Jay screamed at him, rattling the chain. Dr. Cooper hurled one of the carvies. It sailed through the air, spinning like a Frisbee, and hit Jay's forehead with a loud splat. Now Jay really had something to scream about as the venom went to work.

"Look out!" Lila screamed.

Tomás came leaping over the coffin and landed on Jacob Cooper like a ton of bricks, knocking him to the floor. They rolled and grappled and tumbled into gilded battle shields and war masks, which crashed down around them like a chorus of gongs and dinner bells. Tomás was grabbing and clawing and looking for something to bite; Dr. Cooper was just trying to get out from under him.

Lila got into it, grabbing up a candlestick to hit

Tomás on the head. WHAM! He swatted her away with his arm, and she fell against the coffin, hitting her head.

Dr. Cooper saw her sink to the floor, out cold. Then he saw Tomás take a swing at him and blocked it. With a quick twist and a good wrestling hold, he flipped them both over so he was finally on top.

Not for long. Tomás was young, strong, and supercharged with toxin. He threw Dr. Cooper off with one powerful shove, and he went sliding through a pile of gold trinkets.

The air was filling with green dust. Through the green haze Jacob Cooper could see little red numbers blinking across the room: 2:38, 2:37, 2:36.

"Lila!"

She didn't answer. She didn't move.

Tomás came after him again. He used a judo move to trip the man and sent him careening into another stack of gold dishes.

In the excitement, he had let go of the other carvy. Where was it? If he could just get the venom on Tomás . . .

Oh no. He spotted it on the corner of the coffin, happy as a clam, gobbling down the spores and already shifting color from yellow to green. Jay was close to that corner. Maybe he could reach it.

"Jay!"

Jay didn't hear him. He was too disoriented, trying but unable to peel the carvy off his head.

Dr. Cooper dove for the bomb. Tomás dove for Dr. Cooper. They collided before Dr. Cooper could reach the bomb, and they went at it again. Dr.

Cooper threw him off and reached for the bomb. Tomás grabbed him again and threw him over the coffin and into more crashing, tinkling treasure.

1:32, 1:31, 1:30 . . .

Jacob Cooper struggled to his feet, looked everywhere trying to get his bearings, coughed in the green dust, and then spotted the red numbers: *1:20, 1:19, 1:18.* Tomás was coming after him again.

Another head popped up out of the tunnel under the pedestal! Ben Cory!

Oh no. Two of them?

Dr. Cooper shot out his left hand, grabbed the remaining carvy off the corner of the coffin, and prepared to throw it. It didn't resist him. It didn't hiss, or bite, or chirp angrily.

It purred. It was a beautiful, deep green.

I'm sunk, Jacob Cooper thought.

Tomás was half laughing, half growling, slinking like a big cat around the cockeyed coffin.

0:44, 0:43, 0:42 . . .

Ben Cory jumped up out of the tunnel and grabbed Tomás from behind. They fought, they growled. Tomás kicked. Cory hung on. They were busy, occupied with each other.

Dr. Cooper scurried the other way around the coffin and finally grabbed the bomb. *0:30, 0:29, 0:28 . . .*

How do you stop this thing? Dr. Cooper tried pressing some of the buttons on the key pad. He tried cancel, he tried pound and star, he tried 000, he even tried reset. The thing just kept counting down, *0:15, 0:14, 0:13 . . .*

Ben Cory finally got the upper hand, landing a punch to Tomás's jaw that sent him tumbling over the coffin and to the floor, out cold.

Oh great! I'm next! thought Jacob Cooper.

No time left. Dr. Cooper ran for the hole in the wall. Maybe they would survive if the bomb exploded in the hallway.

Ben Cory jumped in his path!

Dr. Cooper braced himself. *You or me, buddy, but this bomb's going through that hole!*

Ben Cory didn't throw a punch. He held out his hand, palm up, gesturing, Let's have it.

Dr. Cooper hesitated, not sure.

0:05, 0:04, 0:03 . . .

Ben Cory grabbed the bomb from his hand, and with amazing skill and dexterity tapped out the correct cancel code.

The display froze at *0:01*.

There was a sudden, eerie stillness. Was it all over?

Ben Cory sighed, then tossed and caught the bomb playfully in his hand. "It's one of mine. I know the cancel code."

Dr. Cooper could just barely feel some relief setting in. "Ben Cory?"

Ben Cory looked at him curiously, cocking his head. "Jake Cooper? What are you doing here?"

"Oh . . . nothing special."

"You look kind of green."

Jacob Cooper chuckled, looking at his green hands. "You ought to see yourself."

Just then, Lila moaned and stirred, rubbing her

head. Dr. Cooper went to her. "Easy now. Don't get up too fast."

"Ooo . . ." she moaned. "What happened? Are we still alive?"

"Dad . . ." It was Jay! "Hey, is that you?"

Dr. Cooper couldn't help smiling as he looked at his son. "Yeah. Is that *you?*"

Jay had finally gotten the carvy off his head and tossed it onto the coffin to join its buddy. "Oh yeah. It's me."

They were alive in the spooky, dusty treasure room of Kachi-Tochetin.

On the plane returning home from Central America, Dr. Cooper tapped out a journal entry on his notebook computer:

We had to confine Tomás until Ben Cory and I could convince Chief Yoaxa to give us a few more yellow carvies for antitoxin. Upon seeing me, Ben Cory, and then Tomás recover fully, the Kachakas began to realize they were not dealing with spooky mukai-tochetin but with a sickness, and they became helpful friends.

With great solemnity, we helped Ben Cory dig real graves, and the remains of John Cory and Brad Frederick were laid to rest in a peaceful setting near the waterfall.

As for Tomás, Juan, and Carlos, the laws in that part of the world were rather vague about what to do with men who have been duped by foreigners and doped by dust, so I doubt they will see much jail time, if any.

The Kachakas found the remains of the man called Manasseh and buried him under the thick, entangling vines of Toco-Rey to be forgotten. We can only conclude that Dr. Armond Basehart perished in the bomb blast that sealed the first tunnel. We never found his remains at all.

As for the deadly curse of Toco-Rey, we consulted a mycologist from Mexico City, who studied the fungus and its spores and discovered it was a whole new species never before identified. The Latin American Mycological Society wanted to name the new species after him, but he chose to give it the name Kachi-Tochetin, after the ruthless king who used it to curse his treasure. He theorizes that the Oltecas knew the carvies carried the cure for the spore toxin and so were able to survive. The Oltecas probably used foreign slaves who had never encountered the spores or the carvies to act as incubators in the tomb, chaining them to the four pillars until the fungus consumed them and filled the treasure room with spores.

The fungus is still there in Toco-Rey and it is still deadly, but the strange flying slugs are also there, keeping nature in balance as they have for centuries.

Happily, the secret of the deadly curse of Toco-Rey is no longer a secret. An international team of toxicologists have begun studying the *slugs and extracting their antitoxin, meaning the spores will no longer be of any use to ruthless weapons dealers.*

The treasure we found has been granted to the Langley Memorial Art Museum in recognition of their past work in preserving the history and artifacts of ancient civilizations around the world. The Langley Museum never really hired us, but I understand they have a bonus waiting for me as a token of gratitude. Nice people.

To conclude, I'll make one observation about all this treasure hunting . . .

Dr. Cooper looked up from his computer keyboard and across the aisle where Jay and Lila sat reclined in their seats, peacefully catching up on some much-needed sleep. Their skin was normal again, and except for some bumps and bruises, they were all right.

Dr. Cooper smiled as he typed,

Having found a fabulous treasure beneath the ground while in the act of saving my two children, I have affirmed one truth I will carry with me for all time: Apart from the dear Lord Himself, my children and my integrity are my greatest treasure, and having them safe with me now, I am the richest man in the world.

An Excerpt from
The Secret of the Desert Stone,
Book Five in The Cooper Kids Adventure Series®

KABOOM! Dr. Henderson's seismic blaster was like a small cannon held in a steel frame and aimed at the ground. When Jay pressed the detonator switch to set off the explosive charge, the device actually leaped a foot off the surface with Jay and Lila standing on it—supposedly to hold it down. Dr. Jennifer Henderson sat calmly in the shade of the airplane's wing, her jacket collar up around her face to block the cold wind, tapping away at her portable computer.

"We should get an image in just a few seconds," she told Dr. Cooper, who was looking over her shoulder. "The blaster sends shock waves through the Stone, and the sensors pick up the echoes. Then the computer interprets the echoes to let us know where the shock waves have been, whether they've passed through rooms or tunnels or different strata of rock. . . ."

The tiny cursor was sweeping back and forth across the computer screen. Line by line, beginning at the top, it was weaving an image like a tapestry. So far the image was one solid field of black. Dr. Henderson started tapping some keys. "Come on, come on . . . don't disappoint me."

"Woo!" Jay hollered as he and Lila hurried back to the plane. "That blaster was some kind of ride!"

Lila was twisting her finger in her ear. "That thing hurt my ears!"

They joined Dr. Cooper and looked over Dr. Henderson's shoulder at the computer image. The black tapestry continued to form on the computer screen as she tapped a few more keys, muttering to herself and scolding the computer, "Come on, don't give me that!"

Finally, the seismic image was complete. Dr. Henderson leaned back, removed her hands from the keyboard, and sighed. "People, unless the equipment isn't working properly, I'm afraid the results are disappointing. The Stone is solid. No rooms, no tunnels, nothing."

"Nothing?" Jay asked, clearly disappointed.

Dr. Henderson shook her head, waving her finger over the image on the screen. "See here? Between the top and bottom surfaces there is virtually no change in density. No cracks. No holes. No gaps or bubbles. Nothing."

"So we haven't progressed much," said Dr. Cooper.

"We may have fallen back a little. We don't even know what the Stone is made of."

"But you said it was basalt," said Lila.

Dr. Henderson shot a glance at the gas-powered core drill lying next to the plane's wheel strut, the drill bit burned and blunted. "While you were setting out the sensors, I tried to drill out a core sample. The drill didn't even make a scratch. If I'm going to be scientific and objective here, I have to admit I don't know what this thing is or what it's made of. I only know it's indestructible."

"Do you still think it's man-made?" Dr. Cooper asked.

Jennifer Henderson sniffed a derisive little laugh. "I'm wondering what the builder used for a chisel. Even though he, or it, or they, left marks, *I* sure can't."

Lila turned her back to a cold breeze that had just kicked up. "His Excellency isn't going to like this."

"Just for my information," said Dr. Henderson, "now that we have the airplane, can't we just fly out of the country from here?"

Dr. Cooper looked across the vast, tabletop surface toward the distant horizon, barely visible beyond the Stone's sharp edge. "Yes, we can. I'm just not sure how far we can go on the fuel we have left."

"Far enough to get out of Togwana would be fine with me."

"But the question is, where can we go? If any of the neighboring countries help us escape, Nkromo would brand them as enemies. I'm not sure they'd want that."

"Well," said Lila, "at least we're safe up here."

As if in response to her words, a disturbing quiver came up through the soles of their shoes.

"I knew it," Dr. Henderson moaned.

The Stone was quaking, all right. Dr. Henderson's computer almost slid off its little stand before she grabbed it. The airplane began to rock, its wings dipping and jiggling. From deep below and all around, there was a deep rumble, like continuous thunder, as a gust of wind whipped across the Stone, kicking up tiny ice pellets that stung their faces.

Dr. Henderson was already throwing her gear into the plane. "Let's go, let's go!"

Dr. Cooper looked to the east and saw a curtain of snow, ice, and boiling clouds coming their way. "Fair weather's over. We'd better get off this thing!"

Lila looked the direction her father was looking and saw the storm approaching. Even so, she insisted, "But we're safe here, really!"

Dr. Cooper just tugged her toward the plane. "Jay, unchock the wheels!"

Dr. Henderson started running away and he grabbed her.

"I've got to get the blaster!" she yelled over the rumble and the wind. "And the drill, and all those sensors—"

"What about the *airplane?*" Dr. Cooper yelled back. "If it gets damaged, we'll never get down!"

The Stone lurched like a bucking horse. The airplane actually skipped backward several feet, and the Coopers tumbled to the ground. The wind began to whip at them angrily.

Dr. Henderson didn't need any more convincing. With a cry of fear, she struggled to her feet, jerked the door open, and clambered inside.

Jay and Lila jumped in the back, Dr. Cooper in the front. The plane was still dancing and side-stepping along the quivering ground as Dr. Cooper rattled off the checklist, his hands flying from lever to button to gauge to switch. "Fuel tanks both, electrical off, breakers in, prop on maximum, carb heat cold . . ."

He twisted the starter switch and the engine came to life, the prop spinning into a blurred disk in front of the windshield.

A blast of wind, snow, and ice hit them broadside from the right. The plane weather-vaned into it, the tail spinning wildly to the left.

"Okay, we're nose into the wind," said Dr. Cooper, jamming the throttle wide open.

The airplane lunged forward, the white swirls of snow and ice blowing past them like sheets in the wind. The old Cessna bucked, skidded, swerved, and tilted as the wind tossed it about, slapping against it this way, then that way. It gained speed, began to tiptoe, then skip along the surface. Dr. Cooper eased the control yoke back, and it took to the air.

"Are we safe?" Dr. Henderson pleaded.

An angry burst of wind came up under one wing and almost flipped the plane over. "Not yet," said Dr. Cooper, trying to hold the plane steady.

Below them, the sharp edge of the Stone appeared to rotate, tilt, rise, and fall as the airplane was tossed about like a leaf in the wind. The Cessna roared, climbed, struggled, clawed for altitude. Another blast of wind carried it sideways.

"Dad, what is it?" Jay asked. "What's happening?"

"Heat-generated updrafts," he yelled over the roar of the engine. "Convergence, convection, wind shear, I don't know—the Stone's affecting the weather."

The plane lurched sideways, twisting, banking, creaking in every joint. A cloud of snow and ice boiled beneath them like an angry white ocean. Dr. Cooper turned the plane eastward, trying to climb above the storm. Below them, the east edge of the

Stone came no closer. The wind was so strong they were standing still!

Then the edge of the Stone began to retreat from them. The wind was blowing them backward!

"Oh, brother," said Dr. Cooper.

"What?" Dr. Henderson cried.

"We're in for a ride. Hang on."

"Can't you do something?"

"If I try to fight against this turbulence, the plane will break apart! We just have to ride it out!"

He eased the throttle back to slow the airplane down, then turned it westward to fly with the wind and get clear of the Stone. The Stone was hidden now beneath an angry mantle of storm clouds, but they could see the clouds breaking over its western edge like water flowing over a waterfall.

"Wind shear," said Dr. Cooper.

"Oh, no," whined Dr. Henderson.

Suddenly, the clouds seemed to suck them down, and they dropped into a nether world of pure white cotton on all sides with no up, no down, no sense of direction.

The altimeter was spinning backward, and they could feel the pressure of the atmosphere building against their ears. Eleven thousand, said the altimeter. Ten thousand. Nine.

They were helpless in a violent downdraft, tossed, twisted, thrown about in the clouds.

Eight thousand. Seven. Six.

And there was nothing they could do, except pray.